HOLLOW HOUSE

GREG CHAPMAN

*T*he stench of putrefaction leaked from the KemperHouse into the air over Willow Street for three days before any of the neighbours noticed it. The residents went about their daily regimen: rising from sleep, going to work and school in the city, renewing the cycle with each dawn, ignorant to the rot growing inside the centuries old house at number 72.

Willow Street never noticed the stink because they'd forgotten the house was even there. The Gothic Revival two-storey dwelling was invisible to them, despite its dilapidation. It was a meaningless edifice of split wood and grimy windows, twisted gutters and a queer metal mailbox overflowing with weeks of junk mail. To its neighbours, the Kemper House had died a long time ago and been left an empty vessel.

They were wrong.

For the ones I love within the Chapman House, Gwenda, Abigail and Leah.

*T*he stench of putrefaction leaked from the KemperHouse into the air over Willow Street for three days before any of the neighbours noticed it. The residents went about their daily regimen: rising from sleep, going to work and school in the city, renewing the cycle with each dawn, ignorant to the rot growing inside the centuries old house at number 72.

Willow Street never noticed the stink because they'd forgotten the house was even there. The Gothic Revival two-storey dwelling was invisible to them, despite its dilapidation. It was a meaningless edifice of split wood and grimy windows, twisted gutters and a queer metal mailbox overflowing with weeks of junk mail. To its neighbours, the Kemper House had died a long time ago and been left an empty vessel.

They were wrong.

CHAPTER ONE

Over those three days during the change from spring to summer, the drift of decay intensified with an almost human determination. The tendrils of death crawled from the Kemper House across the divide to its next-door neighbour, at number 70. The stench seeped through the walls of the low-set 1970s chamferboard house to slowly infect the family that resided there. The Campbell family: Max, aged 43, his wife Carol, 41, and their two sons, Zac, 16, and Matthew, 14. The infection grew as they slept, the fumes pervading their every breath and nesting in their minds—and souls.

Zac was the first in the Campbell family to become aware of the smell. The miasma woke him with the rising sun, and the taste of it was in the back of his throat as he sat up in bed and rubbed his eyes. He glanced, bleary-eyed around his bedroom, in search of the source. There was nothing on the slightly mould-tinged ceiling, and the only things on the walls were posters of his favourite band, *Korn*. He expected to see a stain on either surface, but there was none. His mind now fully aroused by the stink, he scanned the floor, specifically the waste-bin under his desk. He leaned out of bed to peer at the bin's contents and saw it only contained crumpled attempts at the previous night's homework.

As he sat breathing shallow breaths, he felt the skin on the back of his neck crawl. He turned slowly to look out of his bedroom window, which provided an ample view of the house next door—the Kemper House. He walked to the window, his nose following the invisible trail of stench. Matthew thought the house next door looked like a burned piece of meat and he wondered if it was the source of the smell. For several minutes he toyed with the thought of telling his parents, only to realise such an action would involve doing the one thing he hated to do—talk to his Mom and Dad. Instead, Zac resolved to see how long he could tolerate the smell, but he knew it wouldn't be long before it would be impossible for anyone to ignore.

Downstairs, Max Campbell scraped the remnants of his bacon and eggs into the trash bin and swore when he noticed its contents were already overflowing.

"Jesus Christ," he muttered.

"What's wrong now?"

Max turned to see his wife, Carol, scowling at him. He bent over the trash bin and gingerly pulled out the bulging plastic bin liner. Through the opaque plastic he could make out hints of the previous night's meal of burger and fries stewing in their own juices. "The kids never emptied the trash—that's what."

Carol tisked and went back to sipping her coffee while ogling the newspaper. Max was unsure whether his wife was joining him in berating their sons or simply berating him. He didn't know how to read his wife's expressions anymore; the only mood she ever seemed to be in was a bad one. He straightened and felt a twinge in his back. He held the trash bag at arm's length and grimaced.

"Zac!" he yelled in the direction of the stairs. "Come and take out the trash like you were supposed to, last night!"

Carol tisked again. "Do you really have to yell?"

He put his other hand on his hip. "Yes I do have to yell. It's the only way I can get those damn kids to listen to me anymore."

His wife had already returned to reading the news, indifferent to his tirade.

"Zac, are you deaf, boy?!"

Max heard the bedroom door open upstairs and slam a second later. Footfalls dragged along the floor above, and eventually Zac trudged down the stairs like the slumbering un-dead.

"Didn't you hear me calling you?"

Zac gave his father a sideways glance. "Yeah, I heard you."

"So what then, you just chose to ignore me?"

His eldest son reached the bottom of the stairs, his face downcast; he couldn't even look his father in the eye anymore.

He held out the trash bag to his son. "Why didn't you take this out last night, like I told you?"

"I forgot."

"You didn't forget. You were just too damn lazy to do it." He watched Zac frown and clench his jaw. "You got something on your mind, boy?"

Zac was tight-lipped. At least he knew when to keep his mouth shut, Max thought. He shoved the trash bag into the boy's hands. "Now you take that out and don't ever forget to do your chores again."

His son shuffled away through the kitchen and out the back door. Max nodded to himself, proud that he'd reinforced his status with the boy. He'd get Zac on the straight and narrow if it killed him. He turned his attention back to the stairs and wondered where his other son was. Zac might have been absent-minded, but his brother was absent in general.

"You planning on gracing us with your presence anytime soon, Matthew?"

When no response was forthcoming, Max sighed and ascended the stairs, his back screaming blue murder all the while. There was no doubt about it. His sons would be the death of him.

Outside, the smell of the Kemper House hit Zac like a slap to the face. There was no denying that something had died in the house next door, and it wasn't a bird or a rat; he'd seen enough road-kill to know the difference. Flies buzzed about, trying to land on him, as if he was the cause of the smell. Zac swatted them away and ran to the large trash receptacle at end of the backyard, quickly opened the lid and dropped the bag inside. Even the trash bin had a sweeter scent than the house next door.

A blast of the foul air washed over him and he gagged. He ran from it, back toward the relative cleanliness of his own home. He opened the back door into the kitchen and saw his mother standing in the doorway, about to light a cigarette. She grimaced and covered her mouth and nose.

"Aw—is that the trash can?"

Zac shrugged, pleading ignorance.

"What, you can't smell that?" She pushed past him onto the porch and gazed around the yard, hand still clamped over her face. "Smells like something died out here."

Zac made to go inside, but his mother grabbed his wrist.

"Get your father out here," she said, and Zac saw a pang of worry in her eyes. He stood still and his mother raised an eyebrow. "I said, go get your father."

The boy rolled his eyes and about-turned into the kitchen, where he saw his father yelling toward the stairs again.

"Matthew! Get your ass out of bed and come down here for breakfast." Max said. "You boys have to get to school and I need to be at work by eight."

Zac approached, but kept his distance. "Dad, Mom wants you outside."

Max Campbell turned, a scowl twisting his puffy face. Behind him, Matthew dragged his lanky form down the stairs.

"What does she want?" his father said.

Zac shrugged. "I don't know. She just wants you to go outside."

Max grunted. "God dammit. Why can't she just leave me alone?" He stormed by Zac for the door. "You two hurry up and eat some breakfast and clean the dishes. I want you ready to go in twenty minutes."

Zac ignored his father's last salvo and scratched at his hair. "Dad, I was gonna ride to school.

"Fine!" Max said. "Just tell your worthless brother to get his ass moving."

Zac turned to Matthew and gave him a sneer.

"What?" his brother asked.

"Did you sleep with your night-light on again, you big baby?"

Matthew's eyes widened in shame, but he quickly averted his gaze. He shoved his brother aside and made for the fridge. Zac chuckled under his breath at his brother's cowardice and fear; a fear Zac believed was about to be sorely tested by the smell coming from next door.

"Jesus, what is that smell?"

Carol turned to see her husband replicating her expression, right down to the hand clamped over the nose. "I think it's coming from next door," She turned her gaze toward the Kemper House.

"Maybe an opossum or a cat got in there and died?"

"Seems really strong for an opossum."

"A squatter, then?"

Carol coughed. "I think you need to call the police."

Max shook his head. "I'm not calling the cops; I got to go to work. And if there's a dead body in there, I don't want anything to do with it."

She looked over the blackened husk that was the Kemper House. The house had always given her the chills, with its degraded state and eye-like windows. It was an empty house that should have been demolished a long time ago. "Why anyone would think of breaking into that place, I don't know," she said, thinking out loud.

Max had clearly had enough, turning on his heels to head back inside. "Well, I'm not going to stand around out here to wonder why. You call the cops, and let them do all the wondering they like."

As usual, Carol was left to do the dirty work.

Matthew hated how his brother shadowed him. Every day was the same; Zac's stares of condescension, his belittling tone, and the shake of his head. Zac just kept piling it on. Some days his brother's constant criticisms made it hard for Matthew to breathe, but today something else leeched the air from his lungs.

There was a distinct smell in the air, like rotting meat. He wondered if his brother smelled it too. Matthew left his room, grateful that Zac wasn't waiting for him in the hall. He walked to the toilet, urinated, flushed and stepped into the bathroom to look in the mirror. Fear dominated his features; from the grey smudges under his eyes, to the pale complexion that surrounded them. He didn't know why he couldn't control his fear, but the dark—and more specifically the night—terrified him, ever since he'd been a little boy. His parents told him he needed to grow up, to become a man, but he knew something was holding him back, as if he was trapped within his own shadow. Every morning he questioned himself, seeking the reason for his fear, and every morning it grew stronger.

Unsettled by his reflection, Matthew left the bathroom, ready to retreat to the solitude of his room, when Zac stepped in front of him.

"Hey, you smell it, don't you?"

Matthew stared, feigning ignorance.

Zac reached out and punched him in the arm.

"What was that for?" Matthew yelped, clutching his shoulder.

"For being a baby—as usual. Just tell me that you can smell that stink coming from next door."

Matthew shrugged. "Yeah, so what?"

"So it's obvious that something's dead over there. You wanna go and find out what it is?"

Matthew cringed. "No."

This drew another punch from his brother, in the exact same place on his arm.

"Ow! Stop it!"

"Stop being a pussy, will you! There's something really dead over there—possibly a person—and Mom and Dad know about it and are about to call the cops. I wanna get a look at it before the house becomes a no-go-zone."

Matthew tried to get past Zac, but his brother shoved him back.

"Leave me alone," Matthew said.

"Don't you wimp out on me."

"I'm not going. That place could be dangerous. It's been empty for years and the smell is probably some animal that crawled into the roof or something. Plus, we have to get ready so Dad can take us to school."

Zac smirked and shook his head. "I've already told him I'm going to ride to school. Come with me."

Matthew tried more forcefully to get past his brother, but Zac only applied more resistance. Matthew gritted his teeth and shoved his brother against the doorframe. "I'm not going!" His self-satisfaction only lasted a moment as Zac's verbal barbs followed him back to his room.

"Fine, be a pussy then! I'm heading over to take a look. With or without you."

Matthew heard his brother approach from behind, but instead of the expected shove or punch, Zac simply walked back to his own room. Matthew felt the strange compulsion to go after him, to make him change his mind. "Zac!"

His brother stopped outside his bedroom door, turning to flash Matthew a look of indifference. "What, pussy boy?"

He summoned some courage and stood straighter. "Don't go over there. That place gives me the creeps."

Zac chuckled and stepped inside his room, throwing one final barb before slamming the door. "Everything gives you the creeps."

Richard Markham detected the foul smell the minute he stepped onto the porch to pick up the morning newspaper. With a furtive glance up the street towards the Kemper House, he quickly went back inside and closed the door.

He sat at the dinner table in his house at Number 74 Willow Street, dreading another day without sleep, and wondered about the smell that had assailed his senses.

It had been his fourth straight night of insomnia and his 80-year-old body was beginning to show signs of fatigue. His palms were sweaty, his eyelids heavy, his heart pounding against his ribcage. His mind suffered the most, the dream still lingering in his subconscious, like an echo swirling at the bottom of a well. The last time he'd experienced such a nightmare was after he returned from the war. Even sixty years on, the images and faces of the battle were sharp. He could almost feel his skin oozing in the tropical heat and hear the lead tearing through flesh. In the dream's climax Richard was awash in blood, its metallic tang remaining in the back of his throat for hours after waking. The smell coming from the Kemper House was all too familiar. Death was in the air.

Death had been on that battlefield with Richard then, and

it had followed him home, taking root in his mind through dreams and in his body by leaving him sterile. Over time, he had learned to ignore it. But now, as he sniffed the scent of Death, he feared it had taken up residence elsewhere.

The Kemper House had already been on the corner of Willow Street when Richard and his bride Margaret had started to build their house at Number 74 in 1950. He remembered how ancient the Kemper House had looked, a relic of the previous century. It cast a shadow over the rest of the street, and that shadow had deepened as the decades rolled on. Richard wondered how it had remained immune to progress for so long. He struggled to recall seeing anyone coming or going, and it seemed strange now, after all these years of simply being an "old" house, in a relatively quiet street, that Number 72 had finally decided to make itself known.

"Richard?"

The old man turned in his chair to see his wife shuffling up the hall. Her white hair shone like a halo in the early morning light.

"I'm here, Margie," he said, holding his hand out to guide her. Margaret's vision was not as good as it used to be, but her tenacity was as strong as ever.

"Why are you up so early again?"

"No reason in particular; I was just awake is all. I came out here so as not to wake you too."

Margaret held out his hand and Richard savoured the softness of her palm in contrast to the creases on the other side. "You're still having those dreams, aren't you?"

Richard sighed. "There's no fooling you, is there?"

Margaret shuffled by him into the kitchen. She put the kettle on and slowly opened the cupboard for a tea cup. Richard watched her squinting, her once beautiful face full of lines. "You ought to see Doctor Beck about that," she said.

He frowned. "And what exactly would Doctor Beck be able to do about my dreams? He's got plenty of pills for my heart and my water works, but I doubt he's got any wonder drugs for nightmares."

The kettle bubbled as Margaret poured herself a tea. "Well,

if you keep missing sleep, Richard Markham, your old heart might not last much longer." Her slippers scuffed the carpet as she walked to join him at the table.

"I'd get plenty of sleep then."

"And you'd leave me all alone, would you?"

"I'd not be a burden."

"Richard..."

When he saw his wife's lips begin to tremble, he squeezed her hand. "Why do you put up with me, Margie?"

"It's called love, you old fool." She took a sip of her tea and grimaced. "Oh, that's awful."

"What is?"

She put the cup down and pushed it away. "The tea; I don't know... it just tastes... foul."

Richard wasn't a tea drinker; he preferred coffee, and the coffee he'd had when he rose at 4:20 a.m. had tasted fine. The Kemper House crossed his mind once more. "Margie, do you smell something in the air?" He watched his wife's nostrils flare ever so gently.

"Now that you mention it, there is a smell. Like garbage."

Richard swallowed. He'd hoped he'd imagined it, despite his nightmares feeling all too real.

Did you forget to put out the trash?"

"No, no, no—it's not coming from our house; I think it might be coming from that house on the corner."

Margaret's lips made the perfect O. "The Kemper House?"

Richard stood and walked to the front window. Outside, the morning sun was slowly painting Willow Street in golden light. The occupants of the neighbouring houses were still rising, going about their morning ablutions, their quaint cottages and dual-storey facades greeting the dawn. The old man craned his neck to get a better look up his side of the street. He could just make out the roof of the Kemper House, the tiles blackened by the elements.

"I've always hated that house," his wife said.

"Have you ever seen anyone come out of that house?"

"Oh, I don't know. I've never taken much notice of that place."

Richard recalled seeing the postman visiting the house occasionally to deliver the mail, but he couldn't recall ever seeing anyone emerge to collect it. "Do you think anyone lives there?"

"I have no idea," Margaret said. "Can we talk about something else please? I don't want to talk about that house."

He nodded and was about to close the curtains when he saw a police cruiser drive up the street. Quickly, he returned to peer through the glass and saw the car pull up outside Number 72. For a moment Richard dreaded that his nightmares were a sign of worse things to come.

CHAPTER TWO

Zac left without waiting for his brother. He climbed on his BMX bicycle, left the backyard, and rolled along the narrow lane behind Willow Street. He kept his eye on the rear of the Kemper House, the three back windows on the top floor watching him as he passed by. Thick vines from an overgrown bush obscured most of the backyard. The tendrils wrapped tightly around the chain link fence that surrounded the property, but there was no way the barrier was going to stop him from satisfying his curiosity. All he had to do was scale the fence and get a look through one of the windows. He pulled up alongside and peered through. The smell was even stronger at this proximity to the house and Zac was glad he'd skipped breakfast because at that moment, his guts were roiling. He was certain there was a dead body inside, and he needed to be the first person in the street to know about it.

He scanned the lane for people, but all he saw was a grey cat watching him from behind a trash can. He found its yellow gaze unnerving. He looked back to the fence and found a gap between the vines. It was about eight feet high, but still looked like an easy climb. He slipped the tip of his shoe into one of the holes in the chain link and pulled himself up. The fence rocked beneath his weight and the vines rustled. Zac cursed at how loud the rustling was, but he was now committed to get over the top. Straining, he climbed, the skin of his fingers burning from the exertion. His shoes kept getting caught in the holes, but at least his grip was solid. He reached over the top of the fence and looked across at his house. When he was certain he hadn't been seen, he threw his right leg over and jumped down into his neighbour's yard. His shoes slammed into the ground, stirring up a plume of dust and weeds.

The smell was so pungent Zac had to pull his shirt collar over his nose. His knees twinged from the jump, but he willed them to take him across the yard to the back door. He took in the view; he'd never dreamed he'd be this close to it. The exterior was devoid of paint, which allowed the dark, weather-beaten timber to show through. The rough texture of the wood looked like the inside of old bones.

The windows on the ground floor were grimy, cracked and framed with webs left by spiders long dead. He craned his neck to look at the roof. Many of the tiles were missing or broken and the spire on top was bent. The entire house was devoid of colour, as if lacquered with the night itself.

The boy turned his eyes straight ahead and, as he stepped closer, they fixed on the back door. It was closed, but his thrumming heart feared it could open at any moment. Although his shirt filtered some of the stench, he wished he had something for his eyes, which began to water. Ignoring his bodily reactions, Zac reached out and turned the doorknob, only to find it locked. He thought about walking to a window to try and look inside when he realized there was a crawlspace beneath the building. With a wry smile, he held his breath and got on all fours to climb into the belly of the Kemper House.

The neighbours were right to call.

Officers Dawes and Lawson knew the scent when they smelled it; it was imprinted on their brains. The two officers shared a knowing look, that it was indeed death emanating from 72 Willow Street.

"Looks like we're gonna be here for the long haul," Lawson said from the passenger seat.

Dawes examined the house from the comfort of the driver's seat. Parts of the structure of Number 72 were merely dilapidated, while other sections appeared burned. To the officers the stench was as powerful as smoke, yet unseen.

"Hmm..." was all Dawes could say. He hated when these types of call-outs turned out to be right. Dozens of corpses flashed across his mind in a strobe-light effect. He knew Death's aroma and he knew what happened to a dead body when neglected. Seeing a former human reduced to the sum of their parts was the worst part of the job. "C'mon," he said with a sigh. "Let's get started."

Dawes and Lawson stepped out of the cruiser and walked towards the house. Dawes took short, sharp breaths as he studied the property. "That mail looks months old," he said to Lawson, as he noted the piles of junk mail scattered about the base of the mailbox.

His partner frowned at the sight. "Then, why does everything about this place smell so fresh?"

Dawes agreed the newness of the smell was odd, but then so was the house in general. The building was falling apart, almost decaying before their eyes, and for a fleeting moment he considered whether it was the actual house giving off the stench. "You ready?"

His partner dropped his hand to the gun holstered at his hip.

Dawes retrieved the heavy flashlight from his own belt and reached out with his other hand to try the door handle. He called out, "Police!" He pressed his ear to the door. There was only silence.

Lawson leaned in to try and see through one of the filth-caked windows. The boards creaked beneath his shoes. Dawes feared they might both fall through rotten wood. He tapped on the door. "Police. Is there anyone at home?" After another minute of silence, Dawes gave his partner a nod and reached for his radio. "52-60, hold the air for minute. Me and 52-70 are gonna force entry."

The dispatcher's female voice crackled down the line. "Ten-four, 52-60. All units hold the air."

Dawes took a step back, bent his knee and kicked at the front door. The door frame crumbled and cracked, flying inwards to release a great waft of air into the officers' faces. Dawes pressed the inside of his left forearm to his nose, while holding the flashlight in his right. He examined the darkened interior through watery eyes, aggravated by dust and odour. Behind him he heard Lawson coughing, but the noise of his expectorations was drowned out by the buzzing of a multitude of flies.

The officers began their search of the house on autopilot. Dawes' flashlight illuminated millions of dust motes, stirred up by their forced entry. The dust covered everything; the lounge suite with its cracked leather covering, the tattered rug on the floor, the stone-cold fireplace. Dawes stepped quickly, exiting the living room to venture deeper into the building. As he entered the kitchen, the fragrance of putrefaction intensified in waves like a macabre metal-detector. Dawes wanted desperately to take in a lung full of clean air, but he had to go on.

The corpse was splayed out on the kitchen table. There were so many flies and maggots crawling on it that the body seemed to shimmer, a moving feast. The chest cavity had been opened, the angle of the ribcage reminding Dawes of a Venus flytrap. He gasped and sucked in a heady dose of the rotten scent. He wanted to close his eyes, but they were locked on the knife clamped in the dead man's hand.

"In the kitchen!"

As he heard Lawson bound down the stairs, Dawes gingerly reached for his radio once more. "52-60, advise 52-100 we've got a DOA. I'm gonna need Homicide and CSI out here."

The dispatcher's voice pulled him out of his gruesome reverie.

"Ten-four 52-60. 52-100, you copy?"

The officer's supervisor called back. "52-100, ten-four. Show me on the way."

Lawson came to Dawes' side, panting for breath. "Holy shit. I've never seen anything like that."

"You and me both."

Lawson coughed again. "All the other rooms in the house are empty."

"Well, it's Homicide's party now." Dawes finally found the will to walk away from the body. "Check the rooms again and secure the scene. I'll take a look outside." He almost ran out the door, silently praying that he'd never have to step inside that house ever again.

Zac lay flat on the ground beneath the Kemper House and watched the police officers walk around the perimeter, and then back to their car. Fear froze him to the spot, and he realised that scoping out the house had been a bad idea—despite the fact that his assumptions had been right all along.

There was an actual dead body inside the house!

Although the officers' conversations had been muffled, Zac had heard the subsequent radio transmissions well enough. He knew what "Homicide" meant. He watched the two officers get back inside their cruiser and close the doors, probably to get away from the smell. The fact they weren't leaving told Zac things were about to get a lot busier in Willow Street and he'd be best be getting himself gone.

Crawling on his belly through the dirt, he started to make his way back to the rear of the house. His clothes were coated in filth, but he didn't care. He just had to get back home before the police found him. His foot snagged on something and he looked over his shoulder at what was slowing him down. The tip of his sneaker was wedged under something long and flat with a hard edge. Zac pulled his leg muscles taut and the object lifted out of the dirt for a moment before falling once more. Curiosity burning, he turned about to get a closer look at what he had unearthed. Using his hands, he brushed away the loose soil.

The object was a long piece of rotting wood. Zac brushed more dirt away. The piece of timber seemed to be as long as he was. It was barely holding together, and had many markings etched into its surface. They almost looked like words, and despite the wood's obvious age, he believed the markings had been carved by careful hands.

With most of the dirt removed, Zac saw the piece was cut into a particular shape, with a long rectangular half and a shorter, more angular top. He realised he was looking at some sort of lid.

Thoughts raced through his head. Not only had he been one of the first to confirm there was a dead body in the Kemper House, but he'd also possibly stumbled upon a chest of hidden treasure.

Licking his lips eagerly, Zac plunged his fingers under the edge of the lid and lifted. But the lid only rose so far before coming to an abrupt halt. Frowning, he craned his neck and saw there was a large, rusted padlock holding down the lid. At first he thought about giving up on it, until his father's voice emerged in his head.

If it's rusted, then it's weak.

His enthusiasm renewed, Zac scraped away the dirt to expose the lock. He saw it was tethered to the side of the chest, and to his dismay, the rust only appeared to be superficial. And yet, the wood it was bolted to was as soft as the earth around it. Gritting his teeth, he pulled on the lock and its fastener came free with a crack like a branch being wrenched from a tree. The boy's smile widened as he opened the box.

Strangely, the chest was filled only with darkness.

He crawled closer, hopeful that it wasn't empty. He bent over the lip of the chest to peer within and stretched his right arm inside, desperate to feel anything. All his fingers touched was more dirt.

Zac moaned in frustration and began to claw at the dirt, shoving it aside like a dog with a scent. The exertion drew him farther into the chest and before he could stop himself, he fell inside. The lid came down with a thud, and every skerrick of light vanished in an instant. He let out a cry of fright and reached to push it open—only to discover the lid was no longer there.

Confused, he strained his arms in every direction, searching for the walls of the box, but they too were gone. Even the soil beneath him was lost. He seemed to float in a sea of darkness. The boy screamed for help—for the two police officers, for his parents—but his voice no longer carried any weight. Heart pounding fiercely in the black vacuum, Zac tried to move, but it was as if his entire body and all his senses, were totally paralysed.

All but one.

He was granted back his hearing just in time for the screams. They rose softly at first, like the rush of air from the end of a distant tunnel. With each thrum of Zac's terrified heart, the shrieks intensified, octave after octave until the boy's ears—and his very skull—vibrated. Inside the box, Zac's body became a tuning fork until the screams became a message from the centre of Hell itself.

CHAPTER THREE

Voices woke Ben Traynor first, but the reek that assailed his senses as soon as he opened his eyes was like a scream in the dark.

Ben threw back the covers, screwed up his nose at the stench and glanced at the bedside clock on the dresser, next to his dozing wife. The sound of people talking and doors slamming at 7 a.m. was unwelcome to say the least. Then again, he and Megan had only moved into 69 Willow Street two weeks before, and hardly paid notice to anything outside, so it was still too early to judge what could be classed as too noisy. Still, there was no denying the air was rank, and Ben struggled to shake the effluvia from his nostrils as he walked to the window and parted the curtains to see what all the commotion was.

Across the street, he saw half a dozen police vehicles surrounding the house at number 72. He counted the same number of uniformed officers, and long yellow lines of crime scene tape around the property. Other men, dressed in blue overalls and facemasks, carried large plastic containers from the back of an unmarked van. Even a first-day journalist would have known those men were crime scene investigators.

"Jesus! There's a goddamn crime scene across the street."

His wife Megan stirred, her hand pushing a coil of brown hair from her eyes. "What?"

Ben ignored her and returned his attention to the window. Number 72 was just an old house, a ramshackle place he wouldn't give a second glance, but now it was a hotbed of activity. Ben wondered if the smell was coming from inside the rotting walls of the house. The smell—albeit a gut-wrenching one—was good news for any reporter. Where there was death, there was always the chance of a great story.

Megan appeared at his side. "Is it the police? What are they doing here?"

"Look at the tape. It's a crime scene."

"Oh, God, do you... do you think someone's died?"

"Well, it certainly explains the smell."

His wife flared her nostrils, before promptly covering her nose with the back of her hand. "Oh, that's disgusting, and must you be so foul?"

Ben slipped away from her to retrieve his cell phone.

"What are you doing?"

"I'm calling Jacob to let him know what's going on."

Megan folded her arms across her chest. "You're supposed to be on vacation."

"The news never stops." Ben put the phone to his ear, already ignoring her. "The news never stops," he said.

"So why should you, right?" Megan stormed off, leaving him alone.

"The day's already off to a great start," Ben said to himself.

The bathroom door slammed. He hated it when Megan chastised him for doing his job. The phone finally picked up at the other end after the sixth ring.

"Jacob, it's Ben."

"Traynor? Aren't you on vacation?"

Ben smirked and turned back to the circus outside his window. From his vantage point he could just make out a crime scene officer, through a window on the top floor of the old house, taking photographs. "Yeah, well I can't ignore the news when it's going on right outside my front door."

"What are you talking about?"

"Right now, across the street. I've got about a dozen cops and CSI guys going through my neighbour's house. And there's a ripe stink in the air."

"Bullshit."

"Check your police scanner. There's a dead body here in Willow Street, Parkside, and I'm about to walk across the road and get an exclusive."

"No, wait, I'll send a crew to check it out."

Ben shook his head. "Forget it. The story's happening right now and it'll make a great front page. What could be better than having one of your reporters living on the same street as the crime? Besides, you know there's no one better than me to cover it." There was a momentary pause, and Ben could just picture Jacob stroking his salt and pepper beard.

"Fine, Traynor. But don't expect me to pay you any overtime. You're supposed to be on vacation."

Ben smiled. "Come on Jacob, the news is in my blood!"

When Darryl Novak looked at the Kemper House, he felt it look back at him.

He didn't feel afraid when he studied its scarred walls and grimy windows, instead he felt aroused. He could tell the building had touched him and left an imprint, like a piece of grit you can't remove from the corner of your eye. He'd seen the commotion from the kerb and had found his curiosity too hard to resist. He rarely mingled with other people, but the all-too-familiar smell drew him in. Standing amongst the milling crowd, Darryl noticed a man writing in a notebook and fastidiously playing with the buttons on a Dictaphone.

"I had no idea anyone lived in that filthy old house," Darryl said.

The man gave him a sideways glance. "Yeah, me neither. I only just moved in across the street."

"You're a reporter, huh? I've always wanted to meet a reporter." He offered the man his hand. "The name's Darryl. I live up in number 61, the white cottage."

The reporter visibly flinched. He refused to shake his hand. "Uh, yeah… it's nice to meet you, Darryl. Look, I'm kind of in the middle of something."

"Oh, sure, I totally understand. You've got a story to chase. Maybe we can catch up another time? We are neighbours, after all." He flashed a grin, but the man had already started to ignore him.

Darryl licked his lips and let his eyes wander back to the Kemper House. Men in blue overalls mingled at the front door.

There were also a number of police officers within reaching distance, and Darryl decided it was time to leave. He could almost feel the weight of the Kemper House's shadow in his mind as he started to walk away.

Blinking wildly in a bid to shift the house's silhouette, Darryl almost ran into a woman standing on the kerb.

"Oh, I'm sorry," she said. She was tall and lithe, with long curls of brown hair. He hated curly hair.

"It's fine. The name's Darryl." He forced himself to be the gentleman, offered her a smile and a handshake. She never accepted his hand and he saw the corners of her mouth tighten in distaste.

"Megan," was all she said.

The Kemper House pulsed inside his mind's eye; it cascaded down into his groin and he felt himself stiffen. "Sorry," he said, and quickly walked away, the sound of his mother's heckling in his ears.

Ben slipped the Dictaphone into his trouser pocket and pushed through the crowd to get a closer look at the crime scene.

The air was roiling with the smell of decay. The police officers all wore masks, and although Ben wished he had one, he told himself it was all part of the job. His vacation had ended as soon as the smell had touched his senses. Few had the privilege of getting this close to death, and he would use his talents to uncover the truth. He didn't even care that it was so close to home. He knew none of his neighbours and was, therefore, prepared to go out of his way if it increased his chances of getting a better story.

Ben had attended many crime scenes in his five years as a reporter, and he was always entranced by the spectacle of it all. Still, having one right outside his front door was a first, and it was an opportunity he was not about to waste. He approached the uniformed officer guarding the house, doing his utmost to exude confidence, when there was a sudden surge of activity at the front door.

Two forensic officers emerged, wheeling a large black body bag on a stretcher. Their bright blue overalls faded from Ben's vision; all he could see was the sun bouncing off the slick surface of the body bag. The uniformed officer on the outside of the tape had seen Ben approach, but he too was mesmerised by the macabre entourage as it made its way to the unmarked van.

"So there *is* a dead body," Ben said.

The officer recoiled. He held up a hand. "Sir, I'm going to have to ask you to stand back."

"Were they murdered?" Ben's eyes locked on the stretcher as it was collapsed and rolled inside the van.

"I'm not at liberty to say, sir. Now, please step back, this is a crime scene."

Ben pinched his nose. The putrefaction had trailed the body bag out of the house and all the way to the street.

"Hey look, I've seen enough *CSI* to know those guys only wear overalls when they have to handle a dead person." He tried to play it vague, but not stupid and watched the crime scene officers close the doors of the van. The sight of it was etched onto his memory. "Were you the first responder?" he asked.

The officer, whose badge carried the surname Dawes, stared at the van as it drove off.

"Officer?"

The policeman jerked to attention. "Look, sir, this is a police matter, and again, I'm going to have to ask you all to return to your homes."

Ben reached inside his shirt pocket. He retrieved his press pass and waved it in Officer Dawes' face. "Okay, I'm actually a reporter with *The Gazette*. Is there a detective, or a senior officer here I can speak with?"

Dawes frowned. "Sir, any questions or comments will have to go through the department's official channels. Now please, if you could step back."

Ben turned away and kicked a stone across the road in frustration. He grabbed his phone, eager to contact the police department. He looked over his shoulder, and was grateful that the creepy neighbour he'd met earlier had cleared off.

He jogged back towards his house. The whole time, he feared that he and his new wife had moved into anything but a normal neighbourhood.

Amy Cowley watched the unmarked police van drive past her bedroom window at Number 65. Her fears had been confirmed when she saw the body bag, and she felt simultaneously appalled and fascinated. She'd never seen a dead body before, yet the thought of death, and all its aspects, had always been at the back of her mind. Often she'd dreamed of what it would be like, to leave the world, to be dead and gone.

She turned away and reached for her phone. She logged on to Facebook and posted a status update.

Somebody has died on my street.

She waited a few moments to see if any of her "friends" would reply, or even like her status, until her impatience was interrupted by her younger brother Dale, who charged into her room.

"Amy! Amy! Did you see?" His face beamed with excitement. "There's cops all over the place and they just took a dead body away. I knew that smell was really bad."

"You can't just barge into my room!"

Dale's excitement melted. "Jeez, sorry!"

"Just get out of my room!" Amy pushed her brother towards the door.

"Don't push me!"

"Get out!"

Amy shoved him again. She resented his very presence. He was always lurking around her room, sticking his nose in her business. Nothing was private anymore, all because of Dale. If he'd stayed out of her room, he would never have found her journal and her mother never would have found out about why she did what she did. Now, her every thought and feeling was scrutinised and poked—all because of her stupid brother. "Get out you little jerk!"

"Amy!" The girl turned to find her mother standing at the door, her face a fierce scowl. "What is going on?"

Amy quickly hid the phone behind her back. "Dale... he just came into my room without asking..."

Alice glared at the boy. "Is that true? Don't you remember the rule I set about going into Amy's room?"

Dale stood open-mouthed. "I only wanted to tell her about the police outside."

"I have eyes. I'm not blind." Amy interjected.

"That's enough, both of you," Alice said. "What's going on up the street is none of our business. Now, both of you need to finish getting ready for school."

"But Mom," Dale whined. "I want to watch the police some more. It's cool."

Alice pointed out Amy's door. "Go and get ready—now."

The boy stomped from the room and for a moment Amy felt like her mother was on her side. "Thanks, Mom."

Alice's glare hadn't wavered yet. "You need to hurry up as well. Remember you have a counselling session today."

The girl sighed. "I know Mom."

Her mother was already on her way out the door. "Then don't be late. I have to get to work."

Amy dropped onto the edge of her bed and felt tears prick at her eyes. She took a deep breath and urged the thoughts back down; thoughts of failure, ugliness and regret. She knew they could spiral down into darker imaginings if she wasn't careful, so she recalled one of her counsellor's tactics to stay focused, by asking herself questions. But there was only one question which came to mind.

Why is my life so horrible?

The questions rolled in like waves on an abandoned shore.

Why do I prefer virtual friends to my own family?

She put the phone in her lap and refreshed the Facebook screen. One comment had been made on her earlier status: a comment from a name she didn't recognise—*Persona Non Grata*—and she chastised herself for posting her status as Public. She read the stranger's comment and felt sick.

Did you kill them, Amy?

And then her phone screen turned black.

CHAPTER FOUR

Ben kept one eye on his laptop screen and the other on the performance across the street.

It was ironic that a crime had coerced him into taking an interest in his neighbours. Admittedly, he didn't really care who they were, but then who did? Few actually wanted to know who lived next door. Getting to know the neighbours was something people did in the 40s and 50s. Today, people preferred to keep to themselves. Sure, most people introduced themselves when they moved into a neighbourhood, with a casual greeting over the fence, but that was the extent of the relationship. People became strangers because detachment always gave them the impression of safety.

Ben smiled to himself and grabbed a pen to write down that last thought. He thought he might use it in his story. A moment later he looked up from the notepad and out of his window toward number 72 Willow Street. He would never have known the dark house was even there if someone hadn't died inside its walls. Now, he found it hard to look away.

"Irony of ironies," he said to himself.

He chuckled and returned to the keyboard, to bring up a new search page in Google. "Number 72 Willow Street" had several entries, including real estate listings, public records and a mention on the local historical society's page. The state public records showed the house had been built in 1889 by Eric B. Kemper, an architect from Prague. Ben wrote the name down on his notepad for future research.

The slam of a car door drew his gaze back to the street. The first television news crews were starting to arrive. Hopefully a press conference would be staged outside the house and where

Ben could direct his questions to the detective in charge. To get the story, he would need to know who the dead person was and how they'd died. He prayed their cause of death was something more sinister than "natural causes." There was a chance the dead person was some old codger who'd died of a tired heart, but if that were true there wouldn't be so many officers guarding the scene. Something disturbing was happening at 72 Willow Street, and the discovery of a corpse was only the beginning.

Ben ignored the commotion outside and returned to the cache of images on his computer screen. He'd found a number of vintage photographs on the historical society's webpage, and one of them in particular piqued his interest. The faded sepia image was undoubtedly the house across the street, right down to the dark wood and obelisk spire on the roof. According to the text on the site, the photo had been taken in 1932. Sadly, there was no one in the photograph, only the house, obscured by a shard of early afternoon shadow. Ben reached for his notebook again and penned another reminder:

Willow Street, 1932. Library archives?

"Ben?" His wife's voice from the doorway sent a jolt through him.

"Jesus, you scared the hell out of me!"

"I need to speak to you. It's important."

The enigma of 72 Willow Street had him on edge, and any distraction was going to make him lose focus. A bevy of voices rose up from the window. He peered outside to see what was going on. The number of reporters outside the house had now doubled. He felt Megan's voice at his back.

"Ben, please."

Multiple camera flashes strobed inside the front-facing bedroom window of number 72. He would have given his left arm to be in that room. "Do you remember seeing that house when we first came to inspect this place? Or when we moved in?"

"I don't know," Megan said. "I can't remember."

Ben rose and grabbed his wife's arms. Her brow twisted in frustration. "You don't think that house looks like it's straight from an episode of *The Twilight Zone*?"

Megan glanced out the window and Ben watched her blue eyes tracing the house. "It's just... an old house." She looked back to him, and he saw desperation there. "Don't you think what's going on in *our* house is more important?"

"I don't have time for this right now. I have to work. I promised Jacob a story, and the cops are going to call a press conference any minute."

There was a renewed throng outside the window. The media were gathering around a plain-clothes officer.

"Oh, fuck!" He scrambled for his cell phone and Dictaphone.

"I need you to hear me," Megan said. "What are you doing?"

"Babe, I'm sorry. I've got to get this story."

He ran for the door, and from the corner of his eye he saw Megan standing in the middle of the bedroom, her eyes narrowed in anger. All Ben could think of, as he ran down the stairs and out the door, was that if he didn't get the answer to the mystery of number 72 Willow Street, his chances of becoming the reporter he'd always dreamed of were well and truly lost.

Amy's mother, Alice, slammed on the brakes, narrowly avoiding a man who was hell-bent on crossing the road to join the media swarming around the house on the corner.

"Damn reporters!" There was a dozen of them all centred on a man standing on the sidewalk, clearly a detective, or some other type of superior lawman. She negotiated her way around the crowd and kept her eyes on the road, unlike her daughter. "Amy, you shouldn't gawk, honey."

Alice was surprised that something so tragic was unfolding in her street, but like a lot of people, she didn't have the luxury of time to stop and stare. There was too much to be done; one of which was getting Amy to her counselling session. She was glad Dale was old enough to get the bus to school.

When she was certain no one else was going to jump out in front of her car, Alice merged on to the freeway for the journey into the city where Amy would attend her twelfth counselling session. She looked at her daughter out of the corner of her eye. The girl was staring out the window, a blank face peering at a blank world of cars.

"It's going to be hard to ignore something like that, but you're going to have to try," Alice said.

Her daughter flinched, as if Alice had pulled her out of trance. "I was just curious." The girl avoided eye contact by looking at her phone. Alice noticed the screen was blank.

"Is your phone flat?"

Amy put the phone in her schoolbag. "No."

Alice wanted to grab the phone from her daughter's hands and toss it out of the car window, but the counsellor had advised her to continue to allow Amy her creature comforts, so she took a deep breath and followed another of the counsellor's suggestions—to engage her daughter in conversation. "So how do you think the sessions with Dr. Ruskin are going?"

"Fine." Amy's response came far too quickly.

"You just seem a little nervous today, is all." The melee outside number 72 Willow Street crossed her mind. "You know, it was probably just some old person in that house, who passed away in their sleep. Nothing to worry about." Alice slowed at an intersection and tried to study her daughter discreetly. She had to look for signs: was Amy's hair brushed neatly, was she wearing yesterday's clothes? It was always hard to tell when you weren't supposed to notice. She reached out to touch her daughter's hand. "Amy?"

The girl flashed her mother a look of disdain. "What, Mom?"

"You know I love you, and that I only want you to be able to come to me when you're feeling down."

"So you've decided to take the "better-late-than-never" approach?"

Alice felt as though her daughter had slapped her.

"Can we just not talk please?" Amy said through gritted teeth. "I just want you to take me to the counselling session and not suck at trying to talk to me."

Alice opened her lips just as the traffic light turned green and the car behind her honked. She swallowed back her sadness and turned her attention to the road. As silence pervaded the rest of the trip into the city, she wondered if her daughter's precious soul could ever be saved.

After the car almost ran him down as he'd tried to cross the road, Ben decided to wait for the reporters to have their fill. He stood at the back of the throng and watched Detective Baltzer put on a public face. Ben had seen him host press conferences many times and he had a pretty good idea—going by the impatient look on the grizzled detective's face—that it wasn't his favourite part of the job. Regardless, he was surprised to see the veteran detective on this case, given the ongoing missing women investigation.

Ben knew Baltzer wasn't prone to failure. He was one of the best, which meant whatever the police had found inside 72 Willow Street was serious. Baltzer fielded each question with the subtlety of a man who'd done it hundreds of times before. And yet, as Ben watched him answer the reporters' clumsy questions about the who, where, what, why and how, he realised that Baltzer's brave face was just a mask. The way his eyes seemed to dart, and the way he licked his lips, told Ben that there was definitely something strange about this case.

One reporter asked if the victim's identity had been determined, which Ben knew was a completely useless question when the CSI team had only just taken it away. All Baltzer confirmed was that the victim was male. Another reporter, a leggy brunette from Channel 5 asked about the cause of death, which was essentially the previous question, asked in a more ridiculous way. Baltzer was clearly annoyed—or distracted—rubbing the tip of his nose with a finger, repeatedly wetting his lips. Ben knew the detective was a smoker, and the man's urge for a cigarette was almost palpable.

The press conference was about to end. It was time to strike.

"Detective, I have a question." Dozens of faces about-turned to gawp at him. Ben saw the recognition in Baltzer's face.

"Yes, Mr. Traynor?"

Ben thrust his Dictaphone forward and pushed through the crowd. "It's clear this is a homicide investigation. I mean, otherwise, you wouldn't be here, right?"

Baltzer's mouth became a thin line of contempt.

Ben pushed on. "Were there obvious signs of foul play or

that someone had broken into the house?"

The detective shook his head. "There are no signs of forced entry."

"So, the house was locked?"

The media contingent resembled a crowd watching a tennis match.

"As I said, there were no signs of forced entry. Now, if that is all, I have an investigation to oversee—"

Ben nudged closer. The reporters were all looking to him now, and he loved that feeling. "Was the house locked from the inside or the outside?"

Baltzer cleared his throat. "Two officers had to force their way into the house, and the deceased was found inside."

"So, did the dead person lock themselves in or was it the killer?"

It was as if Baltzer was suddenly aware of the cameras. He licked his lips for what must have been the twentieth time. "We're still trying to ascertain that."

Ben asked the right question while he had Baltzer fazed. "Can you give us more details on why the body can't be identified?"

TV cameras pressed in, and the sound of pens scratching into notebooks intensified. The detective stood taller, donning the mask of the seasoned investigator. But Ben saw the truth in his glossy eyes, even as he stared into the nearest camera. "That's all I can say at this time. Once we know more, we'll let you know."

Ben forced his way to the front. "Wait, Detective, I have one last question."

"Mr. Traynor, I don't have time for this."

"No seriously," Ben said. "If the person in the house was in fact murdered, then the killer's still at large, right?"

The reporters turned back to Baltzer, reinvigorated.

"How can the people living in Willow Street—or in West Plains for that matter—feel safe? And can your department handle another murder case when it's already stretched thin looking into the missing women?"

Baltzer swallowed. "I'd like to ask the people of West Plains not to speculate at this point. This is a police matter and we'll be conducting interviews with the residents of Willow Street over the next few days. However, I ask anyone who might have information on this matter to come forward and contact the Homicide Division. Thank you." Baltzer retreated beneath the crime scene tape, back toward the house that was so full of mystery.

Ben didn't have all the answers to his questions yet, but one thing he knew for certain—he had to speak to his neighbours before Baltzer did.

Carol Campbell peeked between the curtains and watched as the media pursued the police officer, throwing a barrage of questions at the man's back. She had no idea what he had said, but something very wrong had gone on inside the house next door.

They really are vultures willing to invade people's God-given right to privacy, all for the sake of a so-called story.

Admittedly, the events occurring next door certainly fit that category, and she expected the media would likely remain outside for quite a few hours, maybe even days.

She leaned forward to get a better look at the officers moving around the front of the neighbouring house. Large standing floodlights beat down on its facade and bled into her home as well. She saw the men in the blue overalls and masks.

They look so alien.

An icy shiver rode the length of Carol's spine. She couldn't believe someone had died mere yards from her house, but even more unbelievable was the fact that someone had lived in that house at all.

She backed away from the window and strained her memory for any clues about her neighbour. She tried to picture whether she'd ever seen them. The only flickers which came to mind were of the house itself, all dark and dank, fleeting glimpses which only served to frighten her. She pitied the poor soul who'd died there, but what sort of a person locked themselves away, estranged from all human contact? It was time to calm down. She plunged a hand inside her dressing gown pocket, searching for her cigarette lighter, and made a line for the back porch.

There was a knock at her front door. Her heart almost stopped.

Tiptoeing back to the curtain, she scanned the porch to see who was there. It was a man, tall and wiry, clad in a drab coat and denim jeans, waiting impatiently at her door.

He doesn't look like a policeman, but then, when was the last time a policeman had come to call?

Given the circumstances, she decided it best to answer. She opened the door, keeping the safety chain securely in place.

The man offered her a wry smile through the gap. "Hello there."

Carol glanced into the street, to see if anyone was watching. "Uh… hello," she said.

The man offered his hand through the gap. "I don't think we've met. I'm Ben Traynor, I live across the street at number 69."

"Oh, hello." She laughed nervously.

Ben Traynor withdrew his hand and scratched at his close-cropped hair. "Well look, I just wanted to make sure you were okay." He turned and nodded at the vultures on the footpath. "I mean, with what's going on and all."

"I'm fine." She couldn't help but wonder why she'd never seen this man before, but then she didn't know anyone was living next door, until the police found a body inside.

"It's just terrible isn't it?" Ben said.

"I'm sorry?"

Ben pointed at number 72. "The dead man next door."

Carol unlatched the safety chain. She opened the door a little wider. "Oh, yes, just awful."

"Did you know him at all?"

"Him?"

Ben smiled. "Your neighbour, did you know him?"

Her eyes widened. "Me? Oh, no. A man, was it? Well, that's a surprise; I thought the place was empty. Like condemned or something."

Ben nodded, and Carol thought he was only half-listening to her. The man seemed pre-occupied. But then he took a step closer, suddenly secretive. "The police are saying that the guy might have been murdered."

"Murdered?"

"Yeah, I overheard the detective telling the reporters. No one knows who the dead person is, the police don't even know yet. I reckon it's because the body's been all cut up."

"Oh, my God." Carol covered her mouth and tried to protect herself behind the door.

Ben's eyes narrowed and his voice lowered. "The media asked if there was a killer on the loose. They wanted to know if the neighbourhood was safe, and do you know what the police guy said?"

She shook her head. Her whole body was trembling. "What?"

"He said they didn't know where the killer was."

The pounding of her heart made her feel giddy. She retreated from the door, and didn't realise that Ben had entered her house until she felt his hand on her elbow.

"Are you okay?"

"I think I need to sit down."

Ben led her to one of the chairs and sat alongside her. "I'm sorry if I've upset you. I just wanted to make sure you were okay and aware of what was going on."

Carol took a long deep breath. "Well, to tell you the truth… I am a little worried now. I didn't think that my neighbour had been murdered. When I smelled that smell—well, of course I knew what it meant—but I still had no idea."

Ben patted her hand. "What's your name?"

"Carol."

"Well Carol, I wish I could have met you under different circumstances and that's the truth of it."

She fought back tears of distress. "It's terrible. I've lived here with my husband and two boys for so many years. Max is my husband. He's at work at the moment and the boys, Matthew and Zac are at school."

Ben nodded again.

Carol could see now he was genuinely interested in her.

"Must be scary though with all that happening right next door while you and your family were sleeping?"

She conjured the house and its darkened rooms, a body all cut to pieces. "It's like… something out of a nightmare."

Ben stood. "Well look, I'm sorry to trouble you. I just thought you should know." He said his goodbyes and left, closing the door on his way out, leaving Carol with thoughts of blood and death.

She watched him leave and was taken aback by the casualness of their conversation. Strange that Ben didn't seem as worried as she was.

Ben strolled away from Carol Campbell's house with a wide smile on his face. He stopped at the kerb and reached into his pocket to retrieve his Dictaphone. He pressed the STOP button. The spools ceased turning.

It was time to turn Carol's fears into a front-page story.

CHAPTER FIVE

The morning's excitement witnessed and curiosity sated, Darryl Novak returned home to indulge in more familiar habits. He pondered the sensations he'd experienced outside the Kemper House as he made himself a rich, mocha latte in his favourite coffee mug. He'd thought there'd been something familiar about the smell coming from that bleak house on the corner. He had to admit, at first he thought the police had come for him. But he knew how to cover up a bad smell. He had skills honed with regular practice; skills that meant he would always go undetected. There'd never be any bad smells coming from *his* house, no sir.

The Kemper House had always had an ominous air about it, and occasionally, Darryl wished he lived inside its walls. The house was indeed strange, but stranger still was his reaction to the woman he'd almost collided with outside number 69. She wasn't his "type" at all. He slurped some more coffee and felt reinvigorated, putting the feelings down to too much sun. He frowned; his mother would have said he had "too much sin on his mind."

Pushing his mother's jibes down, Darryl carried his steaming coffee outside to the backyard bomb shelter. His mother had the shelter built when he was a child. She'd been so anxious about the apparent threat of the Cold War that she'd had to "protect her boy." Darryl clenched his jaw, as his mother's methods of "protection" washed over his subconscious; scolding him, spitting at him, locking him in his room, and when she was very angry, cursing him for ever being born.

He took a deep breath and exhaled slowly. Mother wasn't around to do those things to him anymore. Her house was his and the bomb-shelter, well, it was his man-cave of wonders now. The very sight of it made him lick his lips in anticipation. He couldn't wait to venture inside and indulge in all the "filthy sins" his mother had forbidden him to do when he was young and virile.

Here, the cloying smell of death from the neighbouring house had lost its edge, which Darryl was grateful for, as it reminded him of the dirty work that was an unavoidable part of his extracurricular activities. Making a mess was all part of the fun, but he'd never enjoyed cleaning up, afterwards. He guessed it was a trait which lingered from his childhood. His mother would have certainly said so—if she were still alive.

He crossed the well-manicured backyard, stopping briefly to admire a dazzling white orchid curling from a pot mounted to the fence. It was a thing of beauty, untainted, unsullied. Nature could be so beautiful when it wanted; it didn't need to wear too much make-up or fishnet stockings to emanate a sense of beauty. Nature was honest, unlike the so-called fairer sex.

He reached the shelter door and studied the large rusting brass lock that protected his current most-prized possession. He rifled in his pyjama pants pockets with his free hand and produced the key. As he slipped the key into the lock and turned, he spilled some of the coffee. The liquid scalded his arm. He cursed loudly and almost splashed himself again. The pain plucked his anger like a harp string, and for a moment he thought he was about to lose it.

No, save it up, Darryl. Don't waste it, now.

The shelter door creaked on its hinges, the sound echoing down the stairs into the blackness beneath. Taking a deep breath, and then a slurp from his mug, Darryl closed the door and ventured down the staircase into his den. The darkness closed in, painting his senses in black. He waited a few moments for his eyes to adjust, savouring the smell of his coffee, and the cool touch of the air. Somewhere, a tap dripped, but none of these sensations were as sweet as the woman's sobbing. Darryl followed her music, treading softly in his slippers along the narrow corridor that lead to the main room of the shelter.

The structure was a solid concrete bunker that could

withstand a nuclear bomb blast. Walls so thick a woman could shriek for hours and not a single sound would escape the room. He stood in the doorway and reached up to pull the chain to turn on the light. Incandescent light the colour of piss bathed the room, casting razor sharp shadows onto the walls and floor.

The whore knelt in the room's centre, naked, arms stretched above her head, wrists bound by a steel loop which connected to rusted chains in the ceiling. Her face—which Darryl had painted crudely with stitch-marks of red lipstick and black mascara eyes—oozed terror despite the glare. The red wig he'd put over her ebony locks shimmered in the artificial light.

"You fucking keep away from me!"

Darryl chuckled and took another sip from his mug.

If only mother could see me now, neck-deep in sin.

He ran his gaze over his captive's naked form, admiring the rose and butterfly tattoos curled around her arms and chest, nipples erect against the damp air, black mascara tears encrusted on her cheeks and stitch lipstick smudged with blood from where he'd bitten her. His cock stirred in response, but he wasn't primed yet; he had to make her beautiful.

"Did you want some coffee?"

"Fuck you!" She spat at him.

Darryl smiled and flicked his wrist, soaking the woman with the contents of the mug. The mocha latte splashed across her face and hair. She shrieked and writhed, the scalding liquid turning her face a vivid red. As she squealed in agony, Darryl observed the burning drips as they trailed down her abdomen, leaving bright red snakes of pain, all the way to her pubis.

Darryl's "Raggedy-Ann doll" moaned and tried to shake the excess coffee from her fake hair. Some of it spattered over the real Raggedy-Ann doll that sat on the workbench in the corner. It made Darryl smile to see the only toy his mother had let him play with, subjected to such a "sinful" visual display.

Aroused, he reached into his pyjama pants and pulled out his cock. He began to stroke himself before his captive. Slumped and whimpering into the concrete floor, she never saw him ejaculate, but he knew she would have felt its hot caress.

"Bet you feel all sexy now," he told her. Satisfied with

himself, Darryl left her in misery, with a promise that he would return. Her screams followed him all the way up the stairs into the light of what he knew would be another glorious morning.

Amy sat in her counsellor's cramped waiting room and stared at the blank screen of her phone, desperately wanting it to turn on.

The phone had inexplicably shut down once again, after another Facebook comment from *Persona Non Grata*, despite the fact that her phone had a full charge. She told herself she needed to make sense of the stranger's comment, but deep down she knew it would only feed her anxiety. Frustrated, Amy put the phone back in her bag and waited.

She'd had a dozen sessions with Dr. Ruskin, but each one felt like the first. She looked at the painting on the wall, above the receptionist's desk. The artist had depicted a flock of ducks flying in a V-shape through a cloud-filled blue sky. She caught herself smiling at the thought of being able to soar. Her expression faded quickly. Freedom was a lost cause while her every word and thought were being tested and prodded, as if she were a frog about to be dissected in a school science class. All because of the day she had tried to be free of her cage of misery.

The shrill tone of the receptionist's desk phone brought Amy back to earth and she watched the cheery-faced woman offer her a fake smile.

"Dr Ruskin's ready for you now."

Amy rose and walked the familiar ten paces to the counsellor's door. She knocked, and was invited to enter.

Thankfully, the counsellor's room had space to breathe. Amy liked its ordinariness, with its beige walls and white ceiling. The rug on the floor, bearing countless concentric circles in its weave, was the most colourful thing in the room. She detected a hint of lavender in the air. But what she liked most about Dr. Ruskin's office—there was no trademark couch for the patient to lie on. In its place were a pair of matching stools, with plush leather seats, which she found to be surprisingly comfortable. She sat on one of the stools just as Dr. Ruskin entered the room.

"Good afternoon, Amy."

The doctor wore a smile on her plump face, but carried her clipboard and had put her greying hair into a tight bun.

Was the good doctor about to get serious?

Amy's heart thrummed faster at the prospect. She had always found her counsellor pleasant, but not too probing.

Was all that about to change?

"Hi." Amy said, avoiding eye contact as Dr. Ruskin sat on the other stool. She felt the counsellor's pale blue eyes on her. Ruskin said nothing, which only served to unsettle her more. "Is something wrong?"

"I was just on the phone with your mother."

"My mom?"

Ruskin put the clipboard in her lap and interlaced her fingers on top of it. "Yes, and she mentioned the goings-on in your neighbourhood, this morning."

Amy gritted her teeth; why did her mother always have to overreact? Dr. Ruskin must have sensed her frustration, for she pried further.

"Your mother was concerned the events might be upsetting you."

Amy shrugged, cautiously mindful to manage her reactions. "Someone died in the house down the street, that's all."

"Your mother said the police were involved; that someone might have been murdered?"

"I guess."

"Did it make you feel anxious Amy?"

The girl bit her lip and studied the weave of the rug beneath her; she wished she could dive into its labyrinthine pattern.

"It's okay to talk about it," Ruskin added.

"I don't want to talk about it. It's got nothing to do with me. I didn't even know anyone lived in the house."

"That's understandable. We all live busy lives these days; it's hard to get to know anyone."

Amy tried to offer Ruskin a reassuring smile. She knew where the counsellor was going with the conversation; secrets and lies. "If you want me to talk about how I tried to kill myself, why don't you just ask me?"

Ruskin straightened and opened her clipboard. The session had now officially begun.

"I believe I already know why you tried to take your own life, Amy. I wouldn't make a very good counsellor if I didn't, now would I?" Ruskin's tone had sharpened, which made Amy straighten in her own chair. Ruskin peered at her over her glasses. "You know I'm only trying to help you understand why, Amy, so we can prevent a repeat occurrence."

"It won't happen again." The hairs on the back of her neck stiffened when Ruskin's eyebrows lifted. "Just because somebody died in my street, doesn't mean I'm going to try and kill myself again."

"That's true, but these types of incidences can be enough to bring back memories of when you did try."

Amy stood and plunged her hand into her bag, desperate for her cell phone, forgetting that it wasn't working. "I'm sorry, I just can't do this today... I'm going to call my mom."

Ruskin craned her neck to stare at the phone. "Are you still on Facebook, Amy?"

Amy froze, desperate to keep a blank expression. "Only occasionally."

"You have to be careful."

"I know."

"Remember the real world, the people you live with and talk to each day, are the ones who really matter." Ruskin was starting to sound like her mother.

"I know." Amy said, and she started for the door.

The counsellor's voice followed her. "Amy, the people you try to connect with on Facebook don't really know you like your family. You should talk to your mother. Tell her what you've been feeling."

Amy stared at the doorknob; she was torn between staying and listening and running away. "I can't talk to her anymore."

"Why not?" Ruskin had crossed the floor to stand beside her.

"She doesn't listen. She never has. She doesn't listen to anyone, not even Dad, who she was supposed to love."

Ruskin placed a hand on Amy's shoulder. "Do you honestly

think strangers on the Internet will listen?"

"They do listen! They support me! They never judge me... because they're my friends."

"But it's not the same as talking to someone face-to-face— like we're talking now."

Amy scratched at her hair. "Please... I don't want to talk to her, okay? I don't even want to look at her!"

"Amy..."

"No!"

The girl fled the room, swinging the door wide and racing out. In the reception area, more people had arrived for their sessions with Dr. Ruskin. She felt their eyes on her, the same ogling gazes her mother offered her every day. By the time she made it to the elevator, her eyes were blurred in a flood of tears.

Ben waited until the media crews had thinned out before he ventured back across the street. As the sun began to dip in the western sky, the deep shadow of the Kemper House crawled across the neighbouring houses, a lengthening obelisk of darkness. Ben slinked around the corner into Blake Street, where the west-facing side of the house was cast in a different, more disturbing light. The wood was caked in years of filth, the paint peeling away like a scab. The windows, which had been closed for God-knew how long, had been opened wide by the forensic officers, who were more than likely eager to smell anything but the scent of death. A few of these men were still working inside. Ben would have given his left nut to see the rooms, but sadly his camera would probably be as close as he was ever going to get.

He slipped the Nikon 450 with its 500mm lens out from under his jacket and slowly raised it to his eye. Through the lens, Ben was provided a tantalising glimpse of the room's interior. The walls inside were not much better than those outside. The paint, darkened most likely by dust and a prolonged lack of exposure to natural light, was also peeling in many areas. Yet whoever had lived inside the house had chosen not to address the problem. Instead, they had applied strange symbols and script to every available wall space. Ben twisted the zoom on his lens to get a closer look at the symbols. They'd been painted by a crude hand, little more than scratches. The marks were a dark colour, brown or red. One resembled a hexagon with an inverted triangle inside. Ben snapped a photo of it. Panning the camera to the right, he saw the scribbling of words.

Lidské duše.

"What the fuck does that mean?"

He pressed the capture button over and over, eager for every detail. The house was becoming more interesting than the dead man. When one of the forensic officers noticed him taking photos, Ben quickly lowered his camera. The officer scowled and drew a curtain.

"Shit," Ben said.

Contemplating another plan of attack, he noticed Detective Baltzer exiting the house. Ben figured Baltzer would give him more than he'd divulged at the press conference; he'd done so before. All he had to do was make it worth Baltzer's while. Police provided information anonymously all the time, and Jacob was ready to pull out *The Gazette*'s chequebook if it helped spice up a story, but Baltzer was one of the few cops who wouldn't shirk his personal and professional integrity. Ben crossed the street. "Hey, Baltzer."

The detective was about to get into his car. His bushy eyebrows furrowed. "I don't want to talk to you."

Ben sidled up to him and checked no other reporters could see them talking. "Hey, so what's going on in this place? Is this a murder, or what?"

Baltzer grimaced, opened the car door firmly, got in and slammed it closed. He'd left the window down to abate the heat. "Why would you think I'd tell you anything, regardless of the shit you pulled at the press conference?"

Ben chuckled. "Aw, come on, you know I was just pressing you for facts. That's what we reporters do. We're here to make you look good for the constituents."

Baltzer turned the ignition over. "You're a fucking piece of work, Traynor. That was low, pulling that shit about our caseload."

"Jesus, calm down," Ben said, put off by the cop's stern

demeanour. Usually the veteran detective was more professional. "Look, I can see you're shaken up. What's going on in that house?"

Baltzer pressed the button to raise the power window. "Some fucking sick and twisted shit." He flashed Ben a fiery gaze. "And if you print that in your story, I'll fucking send your ass to jail."

CHAPTER SIX

While police officers kept a silent vigil outside the murder house, Ben returned home in order to put his thoughts into words. He sat on the bed in the master bedroom, with the door closed. He knew there was no chance Megan would enter, but all the same he needed his privacy when work had to be done. It was one of the things that frustrated him the most about his quarrels with Megan; she just didn't understand the work. He played back his conversation with Carol Campbell, transcribed it and then opened a fresh Word document on his laptop. His fingers danced across the keys.

The morbid appearance of the house alone should have served as a warning to the residents of Willow Street, but it was the hideous smell of death that alerted them not all was well in their quiet, suburban neighbourhood.

Ben smiled at his prowess. He was off to a bristling start, but he knew the story needed more scandal. The keys clacked in response to his fingers.

Number 72 Willow Street, a decrepit abode lost to time, finally revealed its secrets yesterday, when police discovered a body inside. Police are yet to determine whether the man, who is yet to be identified, was murdered.

Readers would be hooked, Ben knew it.

One such resident, Carol Campbell, who lives next door to the murder house, admitted she had no clue she had a neighbour at all, until the smell pervaded her home. Also clueless are the local police, who are concerned the man's murderer might still be at large in the city and that the madman might be answering the call of some occult ritual.

He sat back, interlaced his fingers behind his head, and re-read what he'd written. Sure, it wouldn't win a Pulitzer Prize but it was still the heady dose of fictional non-fiction the readers of *The Gazette* expected. He grabbed his phone to call Jacob at the paper. It was just closing in on 6 p.m.

His editor answered on the sixth ring.

"Jesus, you obviously don't want the story of the day," Ben said.

"Traynor? I was wondering when you were going to call. You know we're still holding the front page?"

"Don't lose your shit. I was about to email it, but thought I'd call and give you a taste." He heard the man tell someone to leave the room.

"Okay, okay, let's hear it, but it better be good."

Ben licked his lips. "Okay, get this. I spoke with Detective Baltzer and Christ, I've never seen the guy so worked up."

"Baltzer? They put Baltzer in charge when he's in the middle of the missing hookers case?"

"Yeah, yeah, I know, I brought that up and it really pissed him off. But listen, there's something weird about this one. I got a look through one of the windows, and there were strange words hacked into the wall. Like Latin or something."

"No fucking way. Go on I'm listening."

"This house, Jesus, it's like Amityville meets The Addams Family. You should see it."

"You get photos?"

"Yeah, yeah, I've got photos. But listen, it looks like the neighbours had no idea that anyone lived in the house."

"Really?"

Ben brought up the transcription of his "interview" with Carol Campbell on his laptop. "The next-door neighbour said she had no fucking idea, until the smell surfaced."

"Oh, that's gold. This is going to be a great front page."

"It's on its way."

"Send it direct to Chelsea at the sub's desk and we'll piece it together. Don't forget the photos."

"Fantastic."

"Now, this Carol Campbell—did you get her photo too?"

"Uh, no, I sort of happened to get her story while I was introducing myself. I *am* her neighbour, after all."

"You're joking?"

"Nope, I just happened to have my Dictaphone running as I was talking to her."

Jacob laughed down the line, a guffaw fuelled by tobacco-streaked lungs. "Oh, you sly bastard."

Ben rubbed his bottom lip. "Now listen, Jacob, if you can, keep my byline off this one, okay?"

"Are you serious?"

"Yeah, I don't want the neighbours knowing I'm a reporter, especially if I'm going to keep fishing for leads."

"That makes sense. Just send it through to Chelsea and we'll take it from there."

Ben ended the call and smiled with self-satisfaction. He reached for his notebook once more when he saw Megan standing in the open doorway. There was no look of scorn this time, only disappointment.

"You really *are* a piece of work," she said.

She slammed the door.

"What do you mean, Zac hasn't come home?" Max Campbell tossed his keys onto the table and gaped at his wife who was pacing at the back door.

"What I just said—he hasn't come home from school." Carol peered through the window into the backyard. The police floodlights at the house next door illuminated everything.

Max strode to the fridge, retrieved his dinner of macaroni and cheese, and threw it in the microwave. The muscles in his lower back seized, getting their revenge on him for unduly stretching them beneath the rusted body of a 1987 Toyota Corolla with cracked suspension. "He's probably at a friend's house with what's his name, Toby."

"Tony," Carol said, rolling her eyes. "And no, he's not there. I checked."

Max watched his meal turning in the microwave. He knew

exactly how it felt. "What about Matt? Does he know where he went?"

A pang of recognition crossed Carol's face, and Max remembered that he'd married his wife for her looks (when she'd had them) and not her wits. The microwave beeped out its tones of completion, but he had a feeling his meal would go cold well before the mystery of the whereabouts of his negligent son was solved. He took the meal out of the microwave and stood waiting for his wife to do anything other than worry.

Carol's gaze was locked on the backyard. "I don't know!"

"Have you asked the boy for god's sake?!"

"No!"

Max tossed his plate on the table. "Oh, no don't worry. Leave it to me!"

He stormed out of the kitchen. His steel-capped boots thudded on the timber as he ascended the steps. "Matthew, you get your ass down here, now! I need to talk to you."

The boy appeared from his bedroom a moment later, water beading on his skin, a towel draped around his waist. Death metal music poured from the room. Max eyed the teenager's wet footprints leading back to the shower: one boy absent, the other absent-minded. He needed to give them both a whipping. "Where the hell is your brother?"

Matthew stared at his father. "How should I know?"

"Your mother said he never came home from school." A guitar riff, which sounded more like a cat being put through a tree mulcher than music clawed at Max's ears. "Jesus, can you turn that crap down so I can have a conversation with you?"

Matthew disappeared behind the door and turned down the music. When he came back, Max noticed his son's face wore the expression it always did the moment before he confessed to doing something stupid.

"Sorry..." Matthew said.

"So—where is he?"

"I don't know."

"Bull." Max raised a callused finger. "You know exactly where he is. Is he down at the tunnels again, smoking that goddamn weed?"

Matthew shook his head far too quickly.

"Right, so he's somewhere else then. Are you gonna tell me, or do I have to beat it out of you?"

Matthew gulped. "Dad, I'm sorry, but I don't know where Zac is, honest."

"Honest, my ass!" And now the finger was being pointed. "You get some clothes on, boy. You're gonna take me to where he's at, right now."

Fear, which had always come so easily to Matthew, ever since he was an infant, showed its ugly face again. But Max didn't care; if fear was the only way he was going to keep his two sons in line, he'd serve it up to them in spades.

Max shoved Matthew into his pickup and reversed out of the driveway. The Kemper House blazed with artificial light and swarmed with police.

When the hell are they going to leave?

Matthew stared at the house with that doe-eyed look of terror he always wore.

"So where are we going?"

His son recoiled as if he'd been spooked. "What?"

Max put the truck into drive and started up the street.

"Wake up, boy. We're looking for your dumb ass brother."

"Dad, I told you, I don't know where he is."

Max clenched his jaw and slapped Matthew across the back of the head. "Don't give me that crap. I know you know where he is, and we're gonna drive around until we find him—all night if we have to."

"Dad, why don't you believe me?" Tears welled in the boy's eyes.

Max grunted and turned right onto Blake Street. "You know, you've gotta grow some balls, boy. When I was your age, my dad already had me working at the shop. If I had my way, I'd have your ass out of school and alongside me at the garage. But no, your mother wants to wrap you two up in cotton wool."

Matthew wiped his eyes with the back of his hand. "If you want to drive around all night and waste your time, you go ahead."

Max's knuckles flared white as he squeezed the steering

wheel. He pulled the truck to the side of the road and grabbed Matthew by the scruff of his jacket. "I should beat you six ways from Sunday, you little shit. Now, I've had enough of your attitude. You either tell me what Zac's up to, or I go home and throw all of your shit in the trash!"

Matthew gaped, and it made Max feel in control again.

"Yeah, you heard me. All your crappy music CDs, your posters, your good-for-nothing books, all of them are going to the landfill."

Matthew's fear pooled in his eyes and quivered his lips. "Why are you such an asshole?"

"You keep lying to me, boy, and you'll find out. Now…" Max pulled back into the street. "Now, let's start this again."

Matthew blinked tears from his eyes and wished his father would drive the truck into a tree, or an oncoming car, until he remembered that life wasn't fair, his father couldn't help being a selfish jerk; after all, *his* daddy had raised him that way. Still, Matthew was telling the truth, and no amount of physical or verbal assault from his father was going to change that fact. He'd simply wait until his father realised that.

As Max raved on about the ass-whipping he'd give to Zac when he found him, Matt looked out the window at the darkened neighbourhood. The boy was amazed at how eager people were to remain ignorant of their fear. They were lucky; they could just switch on the television or stare at Facebook and ignore all the bad things going on in the world outside. But to Matthew, fear was like a bug burrowing under his skin or a splinter that just wouldn't come free no matter how much you picked at it.

Until today, he'd never felt the fear so keenly. The Kemper House was to blame, and he knew it. The dead body was the start of something evil. If any good was to come from driving around with his father in the middle of the night, it would be because he was away from that house's influence. Guilt began to assuage him. By getting away from the house, was he leaving Zac to his fate?

Matt guessed early on that Zac had gone over the fence to

get a look at the house next door, and no amount of pleading would have gotten his brother to change his mind. He was more like Max than he realised. Now though, Matt was willingly abandoning him. Should he tell his father what Zac had done? Should he tell him in order to save him?

His arm seared with a jolt of pain. He turned to see his father, red-faced and recoiling his fist.

"Did that get your attention you little shit?"

Matt clutched his throbbing shoulder.

"Are you listening to me, boy?" Max said through gritted teeth. "I said this is your last chance to tell me where your brother is!"

The pain of his father's blow radiated toward his elbow. The nerve-endings jerked in shock. "You can hit me all you want. It's not going to change the fact that I don't know where he is!"

Max punched Matt's shoulder again, in the exact spot as before.

Matt swallowed down the pain.

The whoop of a police siren halted any further onslaught.

"What the hell?" Max pulled to the side of the road.

Matthew watched as two officers stepped out of their cruiser and approached his father's truck. The one closest to the driver's side shone a flashlight in his father's face.

"Is everything all right here, sir?"

Max's demeanour shifted to something more cheerful. "Hey officer, sure everything's fine here."

The other officer gave Matthew a look of concern. "We saw a commotion inside the vehicle."

"Looked like you were striking the boy," the officer with the flashlight added.

Max chuckled. "What? No, I was just giving my son's ear a tweak, you know? The little scamp won't tell me where his brother's hiding. You know what boys are like."

The officer next to Matthew leaned in. "Is that true, son?"

Matthew never heard the officer. His eyes were locked on a shadow standing on the sidewalk, just a few yards from where they were parked. The figure was watching them. Matthew could barely discern the figure's features in the blue-black night, but he knew who it was. His brother Zac was a statue of darkness, standing vigil.

"Son?" The officer said again.

"Don't mind him officer," Max said. "I just put the wind up him, is all."

"You do know there's a heavy police presence in the neighbourhood, sir?" the torch-bearing officer said. "Given the recent incident up the street?"

Max chuckled once more. "Do I know about that? Hell, yes I do. The place where you guys found the body was right next door to me."

Matthew wanted the police to disappear and for his father to take him back home. He felt a rivulet of sweat crawling down his back to his briefs. The silhouette of his brother Zac moved slowly, raising its finger to its lips.

It'll be our little secret.

"Dad, can we just go home, please?" Matthew heard himself say.

"Son, is everything all right?"

Matthew recoiled and looked at the officer who'd spoken to him. When he turned back to the sidewalk, his brother's shadow was gone. "Yeah, it's okay," he said. "Dad's right, I was just being stubborn." He looked to his father, who was squinting at him curiously.

"You should all get on home," the officer with the flashlight said.

Max gripped the wheel. "Yeah, you're right, and I'm sure Zac's back at home now with his mother."

"I'm sure he is," the officer said. "Drive safe now."

The officers went back to their cruiser and drove past them out of Blake Street. Max put the truck in drive and did a U-turn to head back home. He never spoke a word to his son, but his last words to the policeman gouged into Matthew's mind, and he prayed that his father wasn't right.

CHAPTER SEVEN

Amy found solitude in her bedroom. She locked herself away, a butterfly inside a chrysalis of sorrow. Her mother and brother had become thorns in the skin of her psyche and she had to be free of them, if only for a short while.

She lay down on the bed and stared at the ceiling. Remembrances of her session with Dr. Ruskin circled in her mind like vultures. She didn't tell her mother what had happened, and had retreated to the safety of her own four walls. Still, Amy knew that in time, her mother would figure out something was amiss and come knocking with her prying questions.

Everyone wanted a piece of her; everyone wanted her to be normal, but Amy didn't believe she ever would be. Being an introvert and disconnected was part of her, like the colour of her eyes and the shape of her lips. She would always be frail and afraid, until the day she died. She caressed the thin scars at her neck, raised nodes of damaged flesh. Friction burns from the day she'd almost become nothing. If only her mother hadn't come home early. If only she'd locked her bedroom. If only. Thoughts of suicide, although no longer so intense, still lingered like the taste of blood on her tongue. She needed to be free, and she no longer wanted to fail at setting herself free. If she was to attempt suicide again, it had to be perfect.

Cool air coming through the window touched her cheeks and she was surprised to find she'd been crying. She reached up, touched the wetness there, and gazed at it glistening on her fingertips. Before she knew it, she was sobbing. Not from sadness, but rather self-pity.

Amy's phone twittered the tone of an incoming message. She sat up on the bed and reached for her bag, eyes narrowed in confusion. She thought her phone was no longer working. She groped around inside the bag and retrieved the only creature comfort she'd ever really revelled in. When Amy pressed the home button the screen surprisingly came on.

You have 1 new message.

Amy clicked the envelope icon and a photo appeared. The image showed the interior of a house, a living room. She recognised an old tattered leather chair, a frayed rug, a dusty mantelpiece and fireplace, but she had no clue whose house it was. Everything in the room was thick with shadow.

Her phone announced another new message and she almost dropped it.

A second image slid in beneath the first, a fresh playing card from a strange deck. It was another room, full of darkness. Amy tapped it with a finger and the image bloomed to fill the screen. She felt her pulse throbbing as she wondered who could be sending her strange photos and how they had her number.

As she squinted to see the details, she felt like someone in a movie theatre, searching for the aisle. The image had been lit by the faintest of sources. She saw the edge of a bed, the frame of a painting on the wall above it. Scratches, or smears, dark and thick, were scattered about the wall. And as she tried to make sense of the image, her phone trilled for a third time.

You have 1 new message.

It was the same photo, but higher, looking up towards the ceiling. The tips of two black shoes were suspended in the air.

You have 1 new message.

The fourth photo came through seconds later: legs and the hem of a skirt. The skirt looked familiar.

You have 1 new message.

The fifth photo made her scream.

The shoes and skirt were hers. The photos were a patchwork of Amy's body, hardened with rigour, the rope around her neck, a python, curling up to an ornate light fixture on the ceiling of a bedroom she'd never visited. And she was dead, or about to be.

She screamed over and over. The phone left her hand and smacked against the wall. But she never heard its thud. She never heard her mother pounding on the door, or crying to be let in. All Amy knew was the sound of her own voice, denying a death she'd always dreamed of, but never wanted to see.

And yet, someone was determined that she bear witness.

Richard Markham awoke in a sweat, his flannel pyjamas stuck to him like congealed blood. He sat up, drawing in breaths of cold air in a bid to steady his racing heart. It wasn't until his eyes adjusted and revealed he was lying in bed, that he realised he'd been dreaming again. It was the fourth nightmare in as many weeks.

The old man threw the heavy blankets off and put his feet on solid ground. He wiped the sweat from his upper lip. The saltiness tasted harsh on his tongue. He looked over his shoulder at his wife and found her undisturbed. How he wished he could be like her, blissfully unaware of the night. Shivering, he reached for his robe and slippers and got out of bed. His bladder was suddenly awake as well.

Richard shuffled towards the door and reached out to steady himself against the doorframe. The world seemed to tilt as his tired heart tried to cope with being awake at such an ungodly hour. Something pricked the skin of his palm and instinctively, his fingers poked at the doorframe. The paint on the frame crumbled between his fingertips. The entire length of the doorframe was cracked and peeling.

In his half-awake state, he groped at the door and found that it, too, was peeling and dry. A bizarre thought crossed his mind, that the door to his bedroom had been turned inside out, and had been exposed to the midday sun for a hundred years.

Yet it was worse than that.

He stepped through the doorway and into the hall. He felt for the light switch and found only more cracked paint on the walls. Every surface was broken and oozing like sap from a tree wound. Panic set Richard's heart into a fresh, staccato rhythm. He wanted to cry out to his wife, but his voice failed him. His eyes, however, were as keen as they had been when he was half his age. Despite the dark, he could easily make out that he was no longer inside his own home.

Fuelled by adrenalin and a morbid curiosity, Richard

walked along the hall to examine the house that had infected his own. The ragged hallway opened into an expansive living area, with a filth-covered fireplace, a matching lounge suite and a moth-eaten rug. Dust motes, illuminated by a shaft of moonlight through the window in the front door, swarmed like flies so thick, they made the old man want to gag.

His slippers scuffed along the ancient timber floor, as he fought the urge to run for the front door and escape. Would he leave Margaret in danger if he did? He turned on his heels, realising he'd left her back in the bedroom. Yet how could it be, when he wasn't inside his own house? He slapped a gnarled hand across his face. He had to wake up.

Decision made, he started to walk back up the hall, which was now overrun with darkness. He ran his hand along the walls in a bid to find the door, any opening in fact, but all he sensed was a patchwork of peeling paint with razor-sharp edges. He cried out in the dark. "Margie?"

In response, he heard the sound of a chair being scraped along the floor. Richard flinched and about-faced, his body drawn to the vibration. Unable to stop himself, or his thundering heart, the old man walked back into the living room.

There, he found a girl standing on top of a chair, stretching to tie a noose around the chandelier dangling from the ceiling. He knew this girl. It was Amy Cowley, the youngest daughter of Alice Cowley, who lived at Number 65. Amy was so determined in her task, she never noticed the old man until he spoke.

"Amy?" Richard said.

The girl dropped her hands and shrieked at him in sheer bloody fright. The chandelier rattled from the force of it. Richard tried to speak, but the girl's unnatural scream abolished all other sound. The old man dropped to his knees and covered his ears, silently begging for the screaming to stop.

When he opened his eyes Amy was gone, the noose was gone; the other living room was gone. He was back inside his own home, looking like a fool. Relief washed over him. He was thankful to be awake, and safe. He pulled himself to his feet and tried to fathom this latest nightmare. It had been so vivid, so purposeful, almost prophetic.

Released from the terror that had gripped him, Richard's body filled with lethargy, and for the first time, he craved sleep more than reason. He turned to walk the hall to his bedroom, to slip in beside his wife. The smell of pine and sweat invaded his senses. There was another scent as well, one he hadn't smelled for more than sixty years: gun smoke. The hallway evaporated before Richard's eyes and he beheld the jungles of Borneo. He heard a soldier's boots on the jungle floor. His heart almost stopped.

"Kofuku!"

The Japanese soldier's voice was thick with aggression. The old man's knees began to shake, as they'd done in 1943, and yet this time Richard was old and defenceless. His bladder emptied down his leg in a steady torrent of fear.

"Kofuku!"

The soldier demanded that Richard surrender. Sixty years later. In his living room.

"Kofuku!"

Richard felt the jab of a bayonet in his back, and he jerked in response. He turned to face the soldier. The assailant's uniform was dark with blood and sweat, his narrow eyes burning with hatred. Richard raised his hands in surrender, but the gesture was lost in translation. He felt the cold length of steel enter his gullet, an ache that quickly became a blaze of icy pain. He dropped to his knees and clutched his abdomen, desperate to put the bloody coils of his large intestine back where they belonged.

"Margie!" he cried.

He closed his eyes and reopened them, begging for the nightmare to end.

"Margie!"

When he reopened them, the soldier had been replaced by a little boy, young Zachary Campbell.

"Mar... gie!"

The boy pressed a bloody finger to his own smiling lips to shush him.

Reality flickered for a moment. Richard's house was now the Kemper House. His innards were now back in their rightful place, and he realised the nightmare was a message, a sign that he and the boy—and all of Willow Street—were players on its stage.

With the nightmare ended, the old man awoke in the real world, screaming for his wife to kill him.

CHAPTER EIGHT

The sound of the newspaper striking the front door woke Carol with a start. She'd fallen asleep in the recliner, after hours of staring at the front door, praying for her son to walk through it.

"Zac?" She wiped away the crust from the corner of her eyes. "Zac!"

When the door didn't swing wide, tears began to flow. She went to the door, her legs defying her body's weariness. She pulled the door open and looked out into the front yard, but all she saw was a sleeping street and a plastic-wrapped newspaper on the porch. An ache settled in her heart, a familiar fear she hadn't felt since her eldest son was a baby.

The memory of it pushed its way through the cobwebs of her exhausted mind. Zac had been six months old. She'd been at home alone, eight months pregnant with Matthew and Max, as usual, was on the job. She'd just finished feeding Zac when he'd begun to cough. No amount of back rubbing could temper the boy's coughing and within seconds, he'd started to turn blue. She'd never forgotten how his little face had swelled up; his rosebud lips had gaped wide open in search of air. She had panicked and cried out for help, for somebody to save her boy. When he fell limp in her arms she'd run for the phone and dialled 9-1-1. And yet, as she'd screamed her home address to the dispatcher, something had happened. Before her eyes Zac's colour had returned, and the boy had puked all over her. He breathed again. To this day, she believed her son's return to life was a miracle.

Now, standing alone at the front door, she prayed for another such miracle to occur. She picked up the newspaper and wrung it in her hands, surprised by her own strength. She was high on adrenalin and fear. If only she'd paid more attention to Zac, shown him more love, rather than disappointment. He was too much like Max, brimming with vigour and wild abandon, and she wished he'd stayed the sweet little boy she adored in his earlier years, before Max had got his hands on him and filled his mind with engine grease and disrespect.

Max was truly a hopeless man and an even worse father. Distant and then too close, too quick to scold and never caress. His own no-good father had been the same. She never wanted Zac and Matthew to turn out that way, but she guessed it was in their blood, at least in Zac's case.

Matthew was an enigma, timid and wary, like an animal trapped inside a cage. He was afraid of everything and everyone, especially his father. He'd been terrified of the dark ever since birth, and had always wanted to be by his mother's side. In frustration, she'd pushed him away and now the guilt cut deep, for in the back of her mind she'd wanted *Matthew* to be the son who'd disappeared and not the other. Why couldn't Max and Matthew have found Zac? How hard could it be?

"Still no sign of the little shit?"

Max was standing behind her and immediately she felt the desire to slap him. "No." She tried to stay calm.

Max nudged past her onto the porch and looked up and down the street. "Where the hell is he?"

"I think it's time to call the police."

He turned, his face contorted with that ridiculous condescending look. "We don't need to get the cops involved. They've got enough on their plate as it is. You know, with our neighbour being murdered and all."

Carol squeezed the newspaper. "Our son is missing." She could feel her heart racing.

Max gripped her shoulders. "Listen, this little shit's gone to visit one of his friends. They probably just went into the city for a movie or something."

"He's never been out on a school night. He knows he's not allowed to do that."

She watched her husband roll his eyes and shake his head

at her. "Jesus, Carol, he's not a little kid anymore. He's becoming a man. He just wants some freedom like I did when I was his age."

She pulled free of his grip. "He's not becoming a man like you. I won't let him."

"What the hell did you just say?"

He took a step toward her, but Carol wouldn't relent. She pointed the newspaper at him. "I want you to call the police and report him missing. Now."

Max's lips became a taut line. "I'm gonna presume that what you said was because you're all weepy, and I'll let it slide. Like I told you, the boy is out with one of his friends, and you need to calm down and get on the phone and start calling around."

Carol wanted to scream. She threw the paper down and grabbed the cordless phone off the TV table.

"I'm calling 9-1-1."

Max reached out and snatched the phone from her hand. "For God's sake, listen to me!"

"No! I will not! I've listened to you and your crap for twenty-one years and I've had enough of it! If you want to be a decent father, you need to get out there and find my son, or find someone who will."

Carol was shaking, and her palms stung from where her nails had dug into the flesh. She'd never yelled at her husband that way before, and for a moment he stood there looking at her, not in shock, but as if he was simply waiting for her to say something else. She wanted him to yell back at her, because she wanted to yell at him, over and over until he did what she wanted him to do. He took a step forward and lifted his right arm, readying to strike her. She flinched.

"Dad!"

She turned and saw Matthew standing in the kitchen, a look of sheer horror on his face. When she looked back at her husband, both his arms were by his side and he was smiling.

"About time you got up, lazy," he said.

"Dad, what are you doing?"

"Your mother and I are just having a discussion, about Zac."

"You were going to hit her."

Max raised an accusing finger. "Now you listen to me—"

Carol swallowed, and bent to pick up the phone and the newspaper. "Your father and I were talking about calling some of Zac's friends, to see if he spent the night. If you can think of anyone we should call, I'd appreciate it if you'd give me the numbers."

Max and Matthew watched silently as she walked into the kitchen.

"I don't know about you two, but I need some coffee." Carol, hands still shaking, tried to busy herself with a cup and coffee jar. A moment passed before she heard her husband stomp up the stairs and slam the door. Her son, however, lingered behind her.

"Are you okay, Mom?"

"Fine," she said. "Just get me those numbers for Zac's friends."

Matthew shuffled off, leaving her to pour a cup and sit at the table. She stared at her reflection in the black liquid and felt like she wanted to retch. A tear ran down her face, but she was resigned not to let sadness claim her. She reached for the newspaper, looking for distraction, but the front-page headline reminded her that everything within it was too close to home.

STENCH ALERTS NEIGHBOURS
TO SUSPECTED MURDER VICTIM

Once she began to read the story on the happenings right next door, her fear rose anew, as now she'd become the victim.

Ben Traynor cried out when his wife shook him awake.

"There's a woman at the front door," Megan said. "You've pissed her off." His wife left the room without another word.

Ben rose, sat on the edge of the bed, and stared at the alarm clock, while his eyes adjusted to the sunlight streaming in through the bedroom windows. He couldn't even remember going to bed. Everything was a fog after 11 p.m. when he'd eventually turned in his story to *The Gazette*. He guessed he'd had too much scotch.

He stood and pulled on his jeans and yesterday's T-shirt.

A quick glance in the mirror told him he needed a shave three days ago. As he left the bedroom and headed for the stairs, he tried to conjure a woman who could be more pissed at him than his wife. The sight of his neighbour, hands clutched around a copy of *The Gazette*, her eyes narrow with scorn, answered his question. Megan stood on the sidelines, seemingly interested in what was about to unfold.

Ben decided to play the ignorance card. "Uh, hi…it's Carol, right?"

"Don't give me that, you know exactly who I am." She held up the newspaper. "How dare you use my name and statements without my permission!"

Ben heard Megan sigh, and she left the room, which he was silently thankful for. "Hey, Carol, look, I'm sorry, but I don't know what you're talking about."

Carol threw the newspaper at him.

He grabbed it before it hit the floor, and he gave the front page a quick glance. The headline could have been stronger, but at least his photographs captured the gothic nature of the murder house. He put on a mask of shock.

"Oh, my God," he said. "They must have overheard me talking."

Carol folded her arms. "What?"

Ben approached her carefully. "The reporter," he said. "After I spoke to you, I was talking to one of the other neighbours, and these media assholes must have been listening in. I'm so sorry."

"It wasn't you who wrote this?"

"No. I mean, I mentioned that I'd gone to check that you were okay, and that we'd talked about the house and all. The bastards must have recorded me and figured out who you were."

His neighbour took the newspaper back and looked at it anew. "God damn sons of bitches," she said. "I'm going to sue their asses."

Ben slipped his hands in his pockets. "Yeah, you should do that." He saw tears stream down Carol's face. "Hey, are you okay?"

She folded the newspaper and sniffled. "No. My son is missing."

"What?"

She took out a tissue. "He never came home last night. He's probably just up to no good with one of his friends, but I'm worried."

Ben reached out and touched her shoulder. "I'm sorry. I hope he turns up."

"Yeah, me too. I'm not sure if I should call the police."

"Maybe..."

"I mean, if there's a killer on the loose."

The possibility of Carol's son becoming a follow up victim crossed his mind. "Well, I wish you good luck Carol. I can't imagine what you're going through."

She nodded absently and turned to the door. "Thanks."

He ushered her through the door, eager for the conversation, and any further suspicions toward him, to come to an end. He'd have to call Jacob and give him a heads-up about her intentions. When she'd gone, he closed the door and rubbed his eyes, glad he'd gotten himself out of a sticky situation.

"Do you lie with every fucking breath?"

Megan watched him from the entryway to the kitchen. Her eyes were on the verge of angry tears. There were wide grey pools beneath them. She was as tired of him as he was of her.

"Just leave it." He started walking for the stairs.

"Jesus, you just can't help walking all over people, can you."

He sighed and looked her way. "I said, leave it."

She folded her arms, in it for the long haul. "I thought you'd given up the dirty tricks and all that hidden microphone shit."

"Give it a rest. It's my job!"

"And what, that allows you to put your morals to one side does it? Think of that woman and her family, or even the man who died across the street. Do you even care about them or just getting that story?"

Ben approached his wife, heat swelling in his chest. "It's my job, and it always has been. You knew that when you met me— when you *married* me."

The mere mention of their marriage increased the fire behind Megan's eyes. "I never realised I married someone to whom lying came so easily."

"You think I enjoy lying?"

"Yes."

She might as well have slapped him.

"Well, you're wrong. I don't like lying. I don't like having to go to crime scenes and car crashes and burned buildings. I don't like asking people what it's like for their loved ones to die. I lie to them to stay detached."

Megan laughed. "You're not a cop, or a fireman, Ben. You're a reporter for Christ's sake."

"Yeah? Well I may not have to pick up the dead bodies or sift through ashes, but I'm still expected to be there, watching as it happens. If society wasn't so fucking hungry for every morbid detail, I wouldn't have a job to pay for this house, or your weekly fucking shopping sprees!"

She smiled and shook her head. "If you meant one word of that, you'd have quit your job years ago. Tell your bullshit story to someone else, because I'm sick of hearing it."

Ben took a drive, in an attempt to calm down. Willow Street was the epitome of the urban sanctuary, with its pristine lawns, clichéd white picket fences and enviable silence. The house at Number 69 had been the perfect choice; not too old, not too modern, and the purchase price had been a steal. The only downside was that Ben had thought buying a new house would make his wife happy again. He had mistakenly believed that the allure of the suburban lifestyle would reignite a spark of the love she once had for him, but that had clearly been snuffed out years ago.

Rows of houses blurred by. Willow Street was more than ten miles long, stretching north to south, located in one of the oldest and well-to-do parts of the city. For a middle-to-high-income earner, it was the most sought-after suburb for those who wanted to settle down and start a family. He tried to think of the last time he and Megan had spoken about having children. They'd both expressed excitement at the prospect, but then Ben's career had taken a giant, unexpected leap, with a revelation that hit right at the core of local government. A whistle blower had provided documents of unscrupulous land deals between the

Chief Finance Officer and a large construction company. Land previously zoned as being prohibited from development. When Ben exposed the deals in *The Gazette*, the CFO was fired, and had tragically taken his own life before charges could be laid. The story earned *The Gazette* a boost in readership and Ben a new position as the senior reporter.

There was a flicker of guilt on Ben's part about the CFO's suicide, but Jacob told him that it wasn't him who pulled the trigger, so there was no need to feel responsible. After a while, Ben came to accept Jacob's point. Life, as far as his career was concerned, became much busier. Time with Megan involved saying goodbye in the morning and goodnight in the evening. The idea of family seemed so far away. But when a boost in pay provided the opportunity to move out of their flat in the city, and into their own home, Megan seemed amenable, as long as Ben agreed to ease back on work.

He gripped the wheel. Taking a step back from a job that he loved was never going to happen. It wasn't about the money, or the thrill of chasing down the next juicy story. He truly felt he had a duty to everyday people, to inform them of what was going on in their town, no matter how dark it may be. People like him, who worked hard to pay their bills and plan for the future. Sadly, Megan had never shared the same point of view. Now he had a mortgage, a wife who despised him, and a murder mystery right on his doorstep.

As his thoughts brought him back to the Kemper House, his cell phone rang. The dashboard display told him it was Jacob.

"So, how's today's edition selling?"

"Ben, we've had a call from someone who claims to know more about the murder house." Jacob said.

Ben pulled the car to the side of the road. An elderly woman watering her lawn looked at him warily. "Really?"

"Yeah, he says we've got the story all wrong. He says we should be looking into the architect who originally designed the house, not the guy who died in it."

CHAPTER NINE

A lice feared she was losing her daughter all over again.
The signs were all too familiar: Amy withdrawing from human contact and lashing out at anyone who tried to offer her help. Just like before, Amy's phone was the source of her latest bout of despair. This time though, the girl had screamed, opened her door to throw out the offending device, and had barricaded herself back inside her bedroom.

She wished Dale was with her, just to provide another presence, a source of comfort, but she didn't want her son to be drawn into the fray. Alice loved her son, but she needed to protect him, by helping his sister, for all their sakes.

Alice looked down at the shattered screen of her daughter's iPhone and wished Amy had done a better job of destroying it. If Alice had *her* way and fought harder against Dr. Ruskin, she would have melted it to slag the first time. Not only that, she would have tracked down every last one of those online bullies and...

No, she didn't know what she would have done. All she knew, was that she never wanted this for her Amy. She never wanted to have a daughter who hated her own life so much that she was prepared to throw it all away.

She placed the phone on the kitchen counter. The cracked screen resembled a spider's web.

*How fitting. The social network was full of spiders, seeking out
the weak and wounded, while flies that got too close often found
themselves snared.*

She walked away from the phone and approached Amy's bedroom. "Amy, it's me." She reached up and touched the door. The glossy paint was cool on her fingertips. She heard her daughter sobbing and let out a sigh of relief. Silence was Alice's greatest fear. She had to keep trying to help her little girl, to bring her out of the dark.

Flashes of the last time Alice had stood at Amy's bedroom door assaulted her mind's eye; Amy in her school uniform, hanging from the ceiling; shit and piss running down her legs onto the carpet, and the sound she'd never forget—the wet, gasping choke.

"Amy, it's Mom."

"Go away!"

Alice smiled, grateful for her daughter's voice.

"Did you want me to throw the phone away, sweetheart?"

"Leave me alone!"

Alice stared at the door. She wanted the power to see through it, to see into Amy's eyes.

"I can call Dr. Ruskin."

"No! Just stop talking, Mom!"

Alice had to keep trying. "Sweetheart... just tell me what happened?"

"No!" A rush of sobbing flooded her daughter's words. "I don't want to talk about it!"

Alice could sense fear in Amy's voice. This was different. Before, she'd been angry with her bullies, angry at her place in the world, but this sounded like those times when she was a little girl who'd had a bad dream.

"What are you afraid of, sweetie?"

The sobbing became a whimper, barely audible.

"Please, just talk to me."

For several moments there was only Amy's keening. Alice sat against the door, listening. In a morbid way it was peaceful and helped reduce some of the trembling in her hands. There were so many lines in Alice's hands. She was so old and Amy so young. She'd forgotten what it had been like to be a teenager, how much turmoil it could be. She'd forgotten a lot of things since Bob had left her, especially compassion. Deep down she knew she had neglected her children after the divorce. Amy and Dale had become burdens, reminders of the hatred she had towards her husband. The fact he simply walked out of their lives had been a blow to her heart, so much so she'd no longer had any love to give her children. And as resentment ate away at Alice's family, her daughter had become a teenager overnight. The girl only had Facebook to rely upon for guidance. It had led her down the wrong path, with almost tragic consequences. The healing since had been slow and difficult, but Alice wasn't about to let it come undone, now. She closed her eyes and looked into her heart.

"Did I ever tell you about the time my Dad caught me smoking pot?"

Amy's whimpering softened, so Alice kept talking. As she did, she grabbed her own phone and started a text message to Dr. Ruskin.

"I was fifteen, and I'd been going steady with this boy, Reece," Alice said. "Is steady still a word teenagers use? Anyhow, I really liked this guy. He was on the football team and he had the bluest eyes. I wanted to get to know him, and one night at a party at my friend's house, I saw Reece in the backyard, smoking. I knew it wasn't a normal cigarette because it smelled strange. Reece said hello. Smoke was swirling all around him and he offered me a drag. I was prepared to do anything to be with him so I took it. At first it felt like I was... weightless, like there was no gravity. It was amazing—until I started puking all over the place."

Alice heard her daughter sniffling, then the sound of her bed creaking beneath her. The door opened and her daughter's puffy-eyed face greeted her. It was the most beautiful thing she'd ever seen.

"What happened?" Amy asked.

Alice stood, bewildered. "Are you okay?"

"Mom, what happened after you smoked the pot?"

Alice laughed. "You really want to know?"

Amy nodded enthusiastically.

"Well, my Dad wasn't too happy when he came to pick me up. As soon as he got close enough to smell the pot on me, I knew my headache was about to get a whole lot worse."

Amy wiped the tears from her eyes, but her smile washed away every other trace of sadness. "I can't believe you smoked weed."

"Hey, I was a teenager once too, you know." She reached out to take Amy's hand. "I know what it's like to feel alone."

Amy's eyes filled with sadness again, but beneath that veneer Alice could also glimpse understanding. Was she finally reaching some common ground with her daughter? "So, do you want to tell me what happened before, why you smashed your phone?"

Amy glanced downward, tucked a strand of hair behind her ear. "Mom..."

"It's okay if you don't want to. I understand. But if you won't tell me, will you at least tell Dr. Ruskin?"

Fear settled in Amy's eyes once more. She released her mother's hand. "You called Dr. Ruskin?"

Alice raised her hands to placate her. "I'm sorry; I didn't know what else to do. Dr. Ruskin said she can come here if you want."

Amy gasped. "A house call?"

Alice put a hand to Amy's cheek. "It's okay. I can cancel."

"No, don't. I'll see her."

"Are you sure?"

Alice saw her daughter's gaze wander to the phone on the kitchen counter. The girl's eyebrows furrowed in determination.

"I'm very sure." Amy retrieved her damaged phone and walked out onto the porch.

"Amy?" Alice followed her, astounded by the sight of her striding into the backyard, phone in hand.

The girl tossed the phone on the ground and bent to pick up a large rock.

"What are you doing?"

Amy flashed her mother a smile. "Something I should have done a long time ago." She brought the rock down hard. The cracked screen shattered into fragments of plastic and steel.

Alice was left speechless by her daughter's ferocity, and for an instant she was terrified of what had been on the phone to make her daughter act in such a way all over again.

Amy smiled at Dr. Ruskin, and for the first time in her life she had a real reason to be happy; she'd let go of her fears.

"Your mother says you were distressed, that you locked yourself in your room, and just now, smashed your phone? Do you want to tell me what that was about?"

Amy folded her hands in her lap. "Someone was harassing me online, and I just decided to get rid of the problem, that's all."

Dr. Ruskin's eyes narrowed. "You smashed your phone with a rock, Amy."

"Yeah."

Dr. Ruskin moved from the chair and sat next to Amy on the bed. "You say someone was harassing you? What happened, exactly?"

Images of herself hanging from a chandelier in the Kemper House stabbed her psyche. She blocked it out with a smile. "It was just a disagreement, is all," Amy said. "A difference of opinion."

"It must have been quite a disagreement if it made you smash your phone to pieces."

Amy chose her words carefully. "I guess... I guess I finally realised that I had to get rid of the phone."

"Well, that is a big step for you, I'll admit, but it's even bigger step to destroy your phone with a rock. Are you sure you're telling me the whole truth?"

The bedroom suddenly felt smaller. Amy forced another smile. "Look, I'm glad Mom asked you to come over, but I'm fine really. Like you said, I needed to get back into reality."

Dr. Ruskin's gaze softened. "You know I'm here to help you. You seem... different, and I'm just trying to understand why."

Amy pushed a strand of hair behind her ear. "I'm happy."

"I'm sorry, but I think you smashed your phone because you're scared."

The girl swallowed and looked out her window, wanting to escape. Dr. Ruskin was too smart. "I'm scared that you're trying to make me feel sad."

The counsellor's eyes widened. "No, Amy..."

"Well, that's how it feels."

Dr. Ruskin stood and smoothed down her dress. "Okay Amy, okay," she said. "I'm sorry. When you're ready, I'll be happy to hear what you have to say."

Amy smiled at her. "I don't have anything else to say. Thanks for coming Dr. Ruskin."

Alice saw the forlorn expression on Dr. Ruskin's face and felt a pang of sorrow in her heart. The counsellor looked ten years older when she stepped out of Amy's room.

"Did she tell you why she smashed her phone?"

Dr. Ruskin shook her head. "I'm very concerned. This change in behaviour is sudden. She's covering something up."

Alice bit her lip. "Oh, God..."

The counsellor touched Alice's hand. "Let's not panic. Let's just see what happens. You're going to have to monitor her very closely. Right now, she's being defensive, putting up a shield against whatever she read or saw. Sadly, I don't think those shields will hold for very long."

"That god damn phone!"

"Mrs. Cowley, I know how you feel about her having that phone, but as I explained, taking it away would have only isolated her more. Our regimen of monitoring was working; Amy was in control."

"Then how did this happen?"

"It wasn't her fault. Unfortunately, social media is the perfect platform for troublemakers. Have you been monitoring her online usage?"

"Not judiciously. I can't watch her all the time. She only has so much data on that phone and it's timed. I just don't understand what would make her want to destroy it. She didn't do that last time."

"No, instead she did something much worse. Perhaps she really *has* readjusted; perhaps she really wanted to get rid of it."

Alice ran a hand through her hair. The weight of her anxiety was leaving her breathless. "What if you're wrong and someone is out to get her?"

"Well, they can't hurt her online, and the phone is gone. But if anything changes—if she has another anxiety attack—you contact me straight away."

CHAPTER TEN

It wasn't until Ben walked through the doors of *The Gazette* that he realised how much he missed the "buzz" of the newsroom. It was mid-afternoon, so everyone, reporters, sub-editors, and layout artists were frantically putting the next day's edition to bed; so frantically in fact, that hardly any of them gave their star reporter a second glance.

He felt envious of the reporters chained to their desks, their fingers gliding across the keys. They were probably chasing up leads on the murder house, hopefully only the smaller pieces of the puzzle. He'd have to make sure Jacob was keeping him as the lead. He scanned the bull-pit for his editor and found no sign of him. Phones were ringing hot, with a flurry of conversations swirling about the room, all to the soundtrack of the police scanner which sat on a high shelf in the centre of the chaos. How Ben hated and loved that machine.

A hand on his shoulder startled him, and he turned to see Kyle Velechi, *The Gazette*'s sports reporter grinning at him like a Cheshire cat on speed. Ben liked Kyle well enough, but sometimes the guy forgot he was meant to only report on the football jock-heads, not act like them.

"Hey Benji, good to see you man," Kyle said. "I thought you were on vacation, though?"

"Yeah, yeah I am, but with that murder house right across the street, I couldn't resist."

"Yeah, that shit is crazy." He slapped Ben on the shoulder. "Still, awesome story man, awesome."

"Yeah, thanks Kyle, look, Jacob called me in. Have you seen him?"

"Oh, yeah, he's talking to some guy in the boardroom. I

don't know who he is, but he looks like he's on some hard-core drugs or something."

Ben was already walking away. "Thanks." He strode down the hall, waved hello to the photographers editing their images, and almost broke into a jog to get to the boardroom. *The Gazette* had refurbished the executive meeting room the previous year, replacing the walls with glass to visually extend the editorial space. At least, that was the shit the publisher spun to the staff. Ben knew it had more to do with keeping an eye on everyone. At that moment he was grateful for the sneak peek the walls provided him of his potential new source.

The man who'd contacted Jacob about Ben's story looked close to fifty, frail, blanched and unshaven. He was in the midst of a very animated conversation. He wasn't particularly aggressive, more erratic. The look on Jacob's face was one of someone who wished he could be somewhere else, so when he saw Ben staring through the glass, he was quick to cut short his guest's speech, and meet his reporter at the door.

"Sorry I'm late," Ben said.

"Thank Christ you're here," Jacob whispered. "This guy's going on about some crazy shit." He ushered Ben into the room before he could reply. The dishevelled man stood and stared. "This is Ben Traynor, our senior reporter, and he's eager to meet you. Ben, this is Mitchell Cross."

Ben offered his hand. "Hi, Mr. Cross. Thanks for coming in."

Cross didn't accept Ben's handshake; he was too busy wringing his hands together. "You're the guy who wrote the front-page story about the house?"

"That's right," Ben said, frowning. "You told Jacob that you knew something?" The way Cross slowly nodded made Ben wonder if the man's mental faculties were entirely stable.

"I'll leave you two to talk things over," Jacob interrupted before leaving the room without another word.

Ben took a seat at the opposite side of the table, wanting to put as much space between them as possible if things turned hostile. When Cross saw Ben sit, he did the same, but kept on wringing his hands.

"So, what can you tell me about the Willow Street house? Did you know the man who was murdered?"

Cross bit at the fingernail of his index finger, and going by the blood on his fingertips, he indulged in the habit often. Finally, he spoke. "It's not the man; it's the house... or it could be the man."

"I'm sorry, but you're not making much sense."

"The house killed the man—that's what matters," Cross was sweating profusely.

"Did you want a glass of water?"

Cross tapped the table with his bloody finger. "I had a house just like it; the same house."

Ben leaned in. "You used to live in the house?"

"Yes!" He scratched at his brow. "No. No I lived in the same house. On... on another street."

Ben was ready to walk away from this maddening conversation. News stories had the tendency to attract all sorts of conspiracy theorists and unstable minds. Mitchell Cross was looking more and more like one of them with every word he said.

"Mr. Cross, I'm sorry, but I just don't have time to—"

Cross slammed his fist on the table. The reverberation attracted the attention of all the staff on the other side of the glass walls. Ben's instincts told him to run. "You need to listen to me. That... that house... the Kemper House... is everywhere. It destroyed me... my Cindy and my Nathan. It... devoured them!"

"But you said you never lived in that house—"

"It's one of many! So, so many!" Tears streamed down Cross' gaunt cheeks. "My house was just one that... he built. They're all the same." Ben stood, and a fresh wave of panic struck the other man's features. "Wait. Listen, please!" His spittle landed on the boardroom table. "1982. You look it up. Cindy and Nathan Cross. 1982!"

Ben put his hands out in front of him, partly to calm the man down, but mostly in case he had to defend himself. "Okay, Mr. Cross, I think you need to go now, or I'll have to ask Jacob to call security."

Frustration turned Cross' face into a grimace, the veins in his neck bulging. He got to his feet and pointed a trembling finger at Ben. "You need to look into that house... at who built it. Then you'll know why that man died... or didn't! The house has a dark soul! You have to keep an eye on it!"

The man's words were nothing more than babble. "You can rest assured, the authorities are watching that house and trying to find the man's killer. I have a vested interest in this case because I live right across the road."

Cross' face blanched as if he was going to be sick. "You... you live near the house?"

"Like I said, right across the road."

Cross wrung his hands and started to walk around the table. "Then you're in its sights. You have to get away from it. Everyone on the street has to."

Ben backed up as Cross moved around the table bumping the swivel chairs as he went. "Keep your distance." He looked out to the newsroom. Everyone was watching the spectacle. He saw Jacob screaming down the phone.

"That house ... all it wants is blood!" Cross pulled at the sleeves of his tattered coat. "It's his vessel. His temple! It took my family!"

The doors opened and two security guards made a bee-line for him. When Cross saw them he shrieked like someone about to be murdered. "No! No, you must listen to me! It will kill you! Kemper will kill you!"

The guards grabbed Cross' flailing arms. He kicked over chairs and writhed like a snake.

Ben backed away until he hit the wall. Two police officers burst through the door and came to the guards' aid.

All four men brought Cross' face down onto the table. Bloody drool oozed from his lips as he locked his eyes on Ben.

"It will devour you!"

Despite the insanity in the boardroom, Mitchell Cross's mania had planted a seed in Ben's brain, one that demanded he find some sense in the man's words. After the police had taken Cross into their custody, Jacob wanted his star reporter to go home, but Ben couldn't resist the temptation to look into the death of the man's family. He may have appeared mentally ill, but there was no doubting his fear of the Kemper House.

Ben filled a cup of coffee and sat at his desk to scan *The Gazette*'s online archives. He ignored everyone, even though they wanted details of his ordeal in the boardroom. Eventually, all the other reporters, even Jacob, went home, leaving only the sub-editors who were simply too busy to engage him in conversation.

He opened *The Gazette*'s internal archive page, began a new search for Mitchell Cross, and the year 1982. The screen filled with more than two dozen entries. He read the first headline and almost choked on his coffee.

MOTHER KILLS SON, INJURES HUSBAND, TRIES TO BURN DOWN HOUSE

DEC 6, 1982 BY STAFF REPORTERS

A 38-YEAR-old woman is on life support after allegedly slaying her eight-year-old son and attempting to murder her forty-year-old husband in West Plains' northern suburbs.

Police and emergency services personnel were called to the address on Mayne Avenue at approximately 11pm on Monday Night, after neighbours reported hearing screams and seeing flames coming from a window in the centuries-old two-storey dwelling...

Ben continued to read. The second article named Mitchell Cross as the lone survivor and his wife Cindy as the suspected murderer. Cindy died in the hospital less than twelve hours after the incident, from self-inflicted injuries. Police investigators were conducting bed-side interviews with Mitchell, who was suffering from shock. Ben couldn't believe what he was reading. He scanned copies of the hard copy editions of the newspaper for that month, and swore when he caught the front-page of the December 7, 1982 tabloid. The photograph was almost identical to the one he'd taken two days ago of the house across the road from his own. The grainy night shot showed the silhouette of the Cross house, overwhelmed by a cloud of amber flame and grey smoke. The red and blue lights of the emergency vehicles paled in comparison.

Hungry for more, Ben flicked to the December 8 newspaper, which featured a portrait of the Cross family, standing outside their new home. The house on Mayne Avenue was a carbon copy of the Kemper House, right down to the dark wood exterior and needle-like spire. Ben shivered. This was more than mere coincidence, and Ben started to feel that he would have to speak to Mitchell Cross again—and soon.

He pondered the man's bizarre words about the Kemper House; that it had a dark soul that devoured whomever lived within its walls. It seemed preposterous. Ben didn't believe in haunted houses or ghosts, but having two separate tragedies inside two identical houses on the opposite ends of town, albeit decades apart, warranted further investigation. Ben realised he needed to go to the police with this information, but not until he was entirely certain.

He checked his watch. It was closing in on 11 p.m., but he still needed more time. He began a new search, this time in the real estate section of the archive. He searched for any reference to Mayne Avenue, West Plains. Numerous pages appeared, so he narrowed his search by typing in "The Kemper House."

The house had been listed for sale three times, in 1975, 1976 and 1981. The digital scans of the newspaper clippings were identical in description and photograph with the real estate agencies, claiming the "historically-elegant gothic style property was perfect for a family or newlywed couple." Obviously, the 1981 listing was when the Cross family purchased the home, and was troubling, given that tragedy would befall them one year later.

Ben opened a new window in the news archive and searched for "Mayne Avenue, 1975." The result was a copy of the real estate listing. Crossing his fingers, Ben repeated the search for 1976, and his heart began to race when he read the resulting headline:

COUPLE SUES REAL ESTATE OVER SUPPOSED 'HAUNTED HOUSE'

He clicked the link and was taken to a story about Henry and Annabelle Morton, who had taken legal action against McCarthy Property Holdings P/L for failing to properly disclose the house's history.

A second story, six months later, reported that a judge threw out the case and labelled the Morton's claims of paranormal occurrences were without merit. The Morton couple were quoted in the story saying the house had been vacant for more than sixty years before they purchased it in 1976. When Ben rechecked the real estate archive, he read that the house hadn't been purchased or put on the market since the Cross tragedy. Ben made a note that he would have to speak to Henry and Annabelle Morton as well.

His mind buzzing with questions, Ben forced himself to close the screens and shut down his PC. When he stood to leave, a voice behind him left him reeling.

"Are you still here, Traynor?"

"Jesus," Ben said, startled. It took him a few moments to recognise Barry Pearson, one of the senior sub-editors.

"I thought you were on vacation?" Barry shuffled a pile of fax machine paper in his hands.

"Yeah, yeah, I am," Ben said. "I'm just following up on the Willow Street story."

Barry's bushy eyebrows rose. "Funny you should say that," he held up a printout. "The police just sent this statement through."

Ben almost snatched the document from Barry's hands. He read the release. "God damn it."

"Not what you were hoping for?"

He handed the press release back. "They still haven't identified the victim because of the amount of decomposition. It's such bullshit!"

"You think the cops know who the dead guy is?"

"I don't know. It has to be whoever lived in the house, right? I mean, who else could it be?"

"Hey, you're the reporter." Barry walked off toward the editing desk.

Ben grabbed his keys. He needed to rest, but he doubted the

mysteries he'd uncovered would let him. How could he sleep with Mitchell Cross' crazy idea in his head, that the Kemper House would be watching him while he slept?

CHAPTER ELEVEN

Alice sat in her bedroom, examining the fragments of Amy's iPhone and couldn't help feeling they were the shattered pieces of her daughter's soul. The Perspex screen and aluminium frame had been battered into crude shapes by Amy's outpouring of frustration, and nothing Alice could do would put the phone back together.

And yet, she wanted nothing more than to restore her daughter's mental health, the mind of that sweet and innocent girl she'd fallen in love with the first time she'd held her as a babe. Before she'd been exposed to the worst humanity had to offer. In order to have that girl back, Alice knew she'd have to put her daughter's heart back together first.

She rummaged through the pieces of the phone, putting aside the cracked black outer shell, the display screen and battery, in search of its inner components. Amongst the dented metal she found the phone's camera lens, glaring at her like a bloodshot eye. Using a pair of tweezers, Alice searched for the only other piece she was familiar with, the phone's SIM card.

A knock at the door made her drop the tweezers.

"Mom?"

Alice quickly scrambled to return all the pieces of the phone to the clip-seal bag and hide it in one of the drawers. She crossed to the door, opened it, and discovered Amy.

"What were you doing?"

"I was trying to find some change, so we can get pizza, tonight."

"Pizza? You hardly ever want to have pizza."

Alice smiled and grabbed Amy in a hug. "I know sweetheart, I know," she said. "But Dale is on a sleepover tonight, and I thought we could spend some time together." Alice stood back and admired the wry grin on Amy's face. "I just thought it'd be nice to have a bit of a girl's night. We could get some pizza and watch one of those new age rom-com movies you used to like."

"Really? You didn't send Dale away because you want to "talk" to me?"

Alice touched Amy's cheek. "Dale knew that you and I needed some quality time together, so he was actually the one who suggested the sleepover. He does love you. Now go and order pizza while I get some cash together." She gave her daughter a gentle push out the doorway. "And pick out a movie too. Whatever you like. I'm just going to have a quick shower, okay?"

She closed the door. The sight of Amy's perplexed expression made her feel guilty. Alice *did* want to spend time with her daughter, but she also needed to know why the girl destroyed her phone.

After Amy had tried to take her own life, they had made a pact to do everything they could to ensure it never happened again. That included Amy allowing Alice to install internet monitoring software on her phone, and she could now see which websites Amy visited, for how long, without being too intrusive. She had never asked for usernames and passwords to her daughter's Facebook accounts, but now she wished she had. Because then she wouldn't have to scrounge through the remains of her broken phone.

She listened at the door, making sure Amy wasn't lurking in the hall, before she opened her dresser drawer and retrieved what was left of the phone.

Alice breathed a sigh of relief when she found the SIM card was still intact. She opened her laptop and inserted the card into one of the ports. The card's contents appeared in a folder on the screen. She found a single movie file with that day's date and opened it.

Time seemed to stand still as Alice watched the film. The footage was dark and unsteady, revealing the inside of a derelict house. The walls looked as if they were covered in flakes of ash. The operator of the camera was nonchalant, offering only fleeting glimpses of the architecture. Alice had no idea where this house was, and she doubted that Amy would have, either. So, who would have sent such a strange video? Alice knew it was easy enough to click on an unsuspecting file or link. Was that all this was? Alice strained to get a better look. The camera person made a sharp right turn. The view widened to a large living area, and started to ascend towards the ceiling.

But it wasn't until Alice saw the shoes dangling in mid-air that she understood. She clapped a hand over her mouth to stifle a scream, but the tears ran freely. There was no mistaking who the shoes belonged to. Alice slammed the laptop cover closed, but the image of her daughter's bloated face was etched on her memory.

She clutched at her abdomen as a wave of nausea roiled in her gut. Yet the sickness was burned away by a sudden rage. She thrust the pieces of her daughter's phone to the floor, overcome with the same level of frustration and hate that had caused Amy to do the same hours before. Alice swore, letting free an exclamation she rarely uttered. She plucked the SIM card from the reader, ready to snap it in two between her fingers, when a thought emerged through the fog of anger. She still hadn't answered the question of who had sent it.

The SIM card tight in her palm, she retrieved her own phone and fumbled with the casing. A fingernail cracked as she pried her own SIM card free and inserted Amy's in its place.

Many frustrating moments passed as her phone rebooted, but when the screen finally refreshed with the contents of Amy's card, a satisfied smile curled the corners of her mouth. Feverishly, she flicked through the received message log. If she could find the number of the creep who sent Amy the video, then she had something to take to the police. She didn't know how the bastard had managed to put her daughter's face in the gruesome video, but she would make him regret it for the rest of his life.

The beep of an incoming message shattered her resolve. The notification appeared on the screen, and a wave of sickness returned. The sicko was once again peddling his foul wares. Would he ever leave her Amy alone? She opened the message and saw another video file attached.

The video showed a young man, not much more than a boy, standing in a darkened lane. She felt a pang of recognition when she looked at the boy's face that she found difficult to reconcile. The way he smiled at the screen, cold and detached, with eyes sunk deep inside pale skin extinguished Alice's anger in an instant. Somehow, she knew this boy. Was Amy in a relationship with him? Did they know each other at school? While the possibilities flooded Alice's mind, the boy on the screen moved.

Slowly, he lifted his right arm into view, and Alice saw he was holding a length of rope. He smiled a toothy grin, wet and wide. His eyes were unblinking and hungry. The rope was above the boy's head, dangling and coiled in deliberate loops to form a noose. It swung pendulum-like from his plump fist. The noose was a taunt meant for Amy.

"You leave her alone… you little shit!"

She squeezed the phone until her fingers ached, staring at the boy's callous expression. The more she looked at him, the more she remembered. She *did* know this boy She'd seen him many times, from a distance, almost every day.

He was one of the Campbell boys who lived down the road.

Alice gave Amy an excuse that she needed more cash for the pizza, and stormed out of the house. She climbed into the Jeep, reversed out of the driveway, inadvertently screeching the tyres. She was only driving fifty feet, but she had to convince Amy she was going elsewhere. She roared up Willow Street, passing the Campbell house and turned into Blake. She stopped herself from mounting the kerb and driving the Jeep right through the Campbell's front door. Her anger burned in her throat and pounded in her chest. She'd never contemplated taking a life until this moment.

Around the corner, hidden from Amy's view, she screeched to a halt and turned off the ignition. The nearby Kemper House's silhouette cast a long shadow, and she felt its watchful windows judging her. Alice still couldn't fathom how she'd never noticed the house before, but the same could be said about the

Campbells. She hadn't given them a second thought until one of their scumbag children sought to hurt one of her own.

Gritting her teeth, she retrieved the phone containing the incriminating evidence of Zachary Campbell's attack on her Amy. She was going to ram it down his scrawny little throat. She opened the car door and strode across Blake Street and back into Willow. The smell of death still pervaded, like a halo around the Kemper House, like the passing stink of a landfill when the wind changed. Alice pushed thoughts of the murder house aside. Now, there was only its neighbour, the Campbell's at Number 70.

Her feet carried her fury by the neglected gardens on the Campbell's front lawn and along the weed-choked path to the front door. Alice pounded the wood with the flat of her hand, only stopping when the sting became too much. She wanted the boy to answer, to see his smug hateful face contort with fear, the way hers did when she had found her little girl near death.

Another boy opened the door, lanky, long-haired and thin; he was already afraid. The sight of him took the edge off her determination, but only for a moment. She remembered Zachary had a brother, but she couldn't recall this boy's name.

Alice clenched her jaw and stood taller. "I need to speak with your parents—right now."

The Campbell boy frowned. "Mrs. Cowley?"

"Is your mother home?" She looked over the boy's shoulder. "Is everything all right?"

"No, it's not." Alice shoved past him and walked through the door.

"Mrs. Cowley—" the boy said, flustered.

Alice looked around the living room and found it empty. "Carol Campbell? It's Alice Cowley. I need to speak to you about your son. Right now."

The boy came round to face her. "Do you know something about Zac?"

Alice felt her pounding heart. "What? Do you know that he's been terrorising my daughter?"

"Sorry?"

She could see Zac's brother had no clue what she was talking about, unless he was pretending not to know. "Your brother, Zachary. Where is he?"

"I wish we knew," a gruff voice said behind her.

Alice turned to see the Campbell patriarch, Max, standing arms folded. How long had he been there, listening? He smelled of engine grease and sweat, his brow shone with both. Zachary definitely had his father's eyes.

"Dad, she's asking for Zac—"

"Shut up, Matthew," Max said. "Go upstairs to your room so I can have a word with Mrs. Cowley."

Matthew skulked away like a whipped dog. So, Max was the dominating type. But Alice wasn't about to let him walk over her. "Your son Zachary has been sending my daughter disgusting videos."

Max laughed. "Excuse me?"

Alice held up her phone. "My daughter received a video from your son, of him holding a noose. Did he not realise how damaging that could be to Amy's well-being?"

Max stepped forward. "Let me have a look at this video you're talking about."

Alice lowered the phone to her side. "No. I want to talk to Zachary about this, now."

Max's jaw muscles twitched. "Listen here, you crazy cow. You think you can just barge your way in here with these bullshit accusations about my son? I haven't seen Zac in two days. He hasn't come home since they found that body next door. So, if you say you have a video of him, then I want to see it."

Alice's chest heaved with rage and fear. She never expected this. She had only wanted to get the truth. "No. I'm going to the police."

Alice turned for the door.

Max reached out and grabbed her wrist. He pulled her so close she could smell the beer on his breath. "Give me the phone."

Amy couldn't help thinking about the last look on her mother's face. And the way she had left the house, slamming the door behind her and leaving a smear of burned rubber on the driveway was unlike her. Everything had changed, the very moment she'd smashed the phone, and there was only one possible explanation.

Her mother knew.

Amy paced the house, claws of anxiety prickling the back of her neck. How could her mother know about the messages—the photos? She'd smashed that phone until there was nothing left. It was the only thing she could think of to keep it a secret, and yet, somehow her mother knew.

Recalling their earlier conversation, and her mother's strange behaviour, Amy went to into her mother's bedroom, straight to the dresser. She sat in the chair and caught her reflection in the mirror. Her face was white with fear, and just the thought of her mother knowing her secret sent her heart into a terrified rhythm. In her head Amy prayed she was wrong.

She opened the drawer and found only jewellery boxes and bracelets. There was no phone. She searched the top of the dresser, pushing aside hairbrushes and the crystal ring holder she'd bought her mother for her fiftieth birthday. Despite the lack of evidence, Amy couldn't escape the thought that the phone was waiting to be found. In her haste, she knocked a picture frame to the floor. It was a photo of the two of them at Liberty Island, taken a few months before she'd tried to kill herself. As she bent to pick it up, she noticed scraps of metal and plastic in the trash bin.

Amy raked through the bin for the chunks of phone, realising she'd made a grave mistake; she'd forgotten to remove its heart. Where was the SIM card?

Her mother knew.

She held the shattered remains in her sweaty palms.

Her mother knew.

The doorbell rang.

She dropped what was left of the phone and ran to the front door. She had to explain to her mother why she'd kept it a secret, and make her understand she'd finally found the courage to let it all go. She didn't need to worry about what people thought any longer. Living was more important.

She opened the door hoping to see her mother, only to find

a boy smiling at her. It was the boy from up the street. Zachary Campbell.

He was holding up a noose, which he'd fashioned just for her.

CHAPTER TWELVE

Screams drew Megan Traynor to the front window. Through the curtain, she saw little more than silhouettes, shifting in the dark, but she heard a woman making threats about calling the police, while a man stood on his front porch and yelled about wanting to know where his son was. Megan watched the woman run towards Blake Street, climb into her Jeep, and make a U-turn with a long screech of rubber on asphalt. Everyone in the street was going mad.

Megan closed the curtain, but not before she caught a fleeting glimpse of the house directly across the road: number 72, the Kemper House. It stood tall in the moonless night, a dark cathedral. Someone had been murdered in that house, and yet her ridiculous husband saw no sense in keeping away from it. As usual, he only saw the tragedy as another award-winning story-in-the-making. His insatiable appetite for death was making her sick, and there was only one cure.

The spectacle over, Megan turned away from the window and walked to the bottom of the stairs where her suitcase sat, packed and ready. It was time to get away from Ben and his obsessions; from his lies. He thought that starting a new life in a new house would somehow save their marriage, and Megan truthfully had hoped it might be, but she no longer had the strength to try. She was only tormenting herself by staying.

She grabbed her phone and dialled for a taxi but a startling shriek cut the communication before it even began. She was drawn to the curtain once more, her ear trying to discern the authenticity and direction of the sound. Megan didn't have to listen for long as the lone scream became many, long and razor-sharp in the dark. Megan ran to the front door and out into the yard. The cries made her skin crawl.

"Someone help me! Help me!"

The screams were coming from one of the neighbouring houses, number 65; she recognised the Jeep she'd seen earlier in the driveway, its headlights still on and the driver's side door wide open.

"No! Amy!"

Megan's feet and curiosity carried her closer to the place she didn't want to go. Instinctively, she looked to her phone, ready to dial 9-1-1. For a fleeting moment she wished she had Ben by her side.

"Amy!" Amyyyyy!"

She was now close enough to smell the Jeep's exhaust fumes, to feel the woman's terror, and know something was terribly wrong. Megan stopped and thought to call out and offer help, but her instinct kicked in anew, advising her to be wary. As she argued with herself, the decision was made for her when the screaming woman ran out the front door in Megan's direction.

"Please help me! It's my daughter!"

Megan put her arms out to keep the hysterical woman at a distance. "What's wrong?"

"My daughter … please! Help me!" The woman grabbed Megan's arm and tried to pull her inside.

"What's happened?"

"Please—she's dying!"

"What's happened?"

"She's tried to kill herself! Please you have to help me!"

"Have you called for an ambulance?" Megan pulled away and dialled 9-1-1.

The woman latched on to her arm once more, fingernails digging through her sweater. Megan complied, staggering through the doorway as the call went through to the dispatcher. The woman's daughter lay on the living room floor, eyes wide open and locked on the ceiling. The noose coiled next to her was like a sleeping serpent. It had left its distinctive mark on the girl's milky-white throat.

"9-1-1, what's your emergency?" the dispatcher said.

Megan closed her eyes. "A girl… a girl's tried to…" she said as the girl's mother went to her knees and screamed her name. "A girl is dead…"

Megan knew she was right; the people in the street were going mad to the point of death.

Blue and red emergency lights painted the sidewalks and houses of Willow Street for the second time in as many days. As Ben stared at them he wondered if they would ever prevail against the black night.

He stood with his wife outside number 65 and watched the frenetic performance of paramedics and police officers as they went about their business, taking the body of the young girl away. The spectacle had drawn many people out of their homes; an audience to death, to one woman's misery.

Megan had told Ben the woman's name was Alice and the girl's name was Amy. She'd followed Alice's screams and been the one to call 9-1-1. That's all the two of them had said to each other since he'd gotten back from *The Gazette*. Other onlookers whispered and pointed, not knowing the true value of silence when Death came calling. Ben observed them, and remembered the first time he'd covered a suburban death; a man who'd died from a heart attack in the middle of summer, slowly but surely letting his death be known. Not unlike the way the murder house had done. He recalled talking to the neighbours over their pickets fences as the flies had buzzed, and how quick they were to claim they knew all there was to know about the dead man.

Ben hardly knew anyone on the street where he lived, although he flinched when his eyes locked on to the familiar face of Carol Campbell. He knew her well enough. She looked right at him, eyes brimming with scorn. He avoided her gaze, opting to look at his wife, instead. "We should go," he said.

"Aren't you going to call the paper?" Megan's voice was thick with condescension. "You called Jacob when they found that man murdered across the street."

Ben sighed. "You want to do this now, in front of all these people?"

Megan faced him and in the blue and red light, her sorrowful face suddenly beautiful. "I didn't even know who these people were until this shit happened to them."

He reached to take her arm, but thought better of it. "Come on, let's go home."

They turned to watch as two police officers escorted Alice to a patrol car. She was hunched and sobbing. The red and blue lights started to move out of Willow Street, a colourful procession of tragedy.

"Where were you?" Megan asked, as they turned to walk back home.

"*At* The Gazette."

She stopped and gave him a frown of disbelief,

"There was a guy there who knew something about the house."

"Just… just… don't talk to me…"

Silence followed them back to number 69.

Carol Campbell didn't know what would tear her heart in two first—rage or grief.

The look on Alice Cowley's face, having discovered her daughter's body, left Carol reeling. Only moments before she'd been in Carol's house screaming at Max, something about Zachary.

Carol had been resting when the confrontation began, and when Max had stubbornly refused to reveal the nature of the argument, she had run up the street to try and get the details from the woman herself. Now, Carol felt numb, while the death of the girl ignited new fears about her son and where he could be.

As the gawkers, including that unscrupulous Ben Traynor and his wife from across the street, finally began to disperse, Carol tried to recall whether she'd ever spoken to Alice Cowley. She was sure Alice and her daughter had lived down the street for as long as her own family had, but only occasionally had they shared looks and smiles. Apart from that, they'd had no contact. Carol wrapped her arms around herself and glanced at the darkened faces of her neighbours as they walked away. They were all strangers, complete strangers. Was it fear that kept neighbours apart, or apathy? Carol didn't know, but since the discovery of the dead man in that godforsaken house, she now wondered who lived next door and what they were up to.

She began to walk home, preparing to grill her husband about his talk with Alice Cowley. She'd find out where her son was, if it killed her.

As the ambulance rolled by Number 74, Margaret Markham said a silent prayer for Alice and Amy Cowley. From the number of police cars and people milling about in the street, Margaret knew something terrible had happened at the Cowley house. Even with her failing eyesight, she knew by Alice's Cowley's screams that whatever it was involved her little girl.

It was the second tragedy to occur since the awfulness at the Kemper House, and somehow she knew the house was had something to do with it.

First the dead man, and now the Cowley girl. Its infectious nature was spreading, to claim lives young and old.

She left the window and returned as quickly as she could to her bedroom, to be by her husband Richard's side. She found him listless, his skin hot and shining with sweat. If it wasn't for the sharp intake of breath through his open mouth, she would have believed him already dead. She took his hand.

"Richard... darling..." she said. "I think... I think the Cowley girl... I think she's gone. I need you to hold on."

Richard managed to open his eyes. "You... need... to get away..."

Margaret shook her head. "No, I'm staying with you."

He squeezed her hand, but there was no strength in his fingers. "That house..." his voice grated. "...it's sick. It'll make you... sick too."

Margaret smoothed down her husband's hair, the skin beneath like fire. His throat pulsed with hot blood. "I'm going to call Dr. Beck," she said.

Richard didn't respond and she realised he'd passed out again. She reached for the cordless phone and their book of phone numbers on the dresser, and dialled Dr. Beck's surgery, only to realise that it was almost midnight. She put the phone back in its cradle, and immediately it rang, startling her. She answered it quickly so the noise wouldn't wake her husband.

"Huh... Hello?"

The other end of the line crackled, like cellophane being crushed.

"Hello?"

Margaret wondered who would call at almost midnight: a wrong number, or a telemarketer? Their phone hardly ever rang at all, let alone in the dead of night. She was moving the phone away from her ear when a voice broke through the static.

"Margaret..."

Her heart quickened; it was Richard talking.

"Ri...Richard?" She looked at her husband lying unmoving on the bed.

"Margaret..." the voice said. "You need to get away..."

Margaret backed away from her husband.

"You need to get away..." the voice continued, "...because I'm going to kill you."

The old woman dropped the phone and screamed, but not even that would wake her husband. Neither did the laughter coming out of the phone.

There were too many people out tonight, Darryl thought, too much noise.

He was glad the sirens and emergency lights had gone. Obviously, something had gone down at number 65, but he only cared because it distracted him from his work. Peace and quiet, his mother would have said, had she still been alive, peace and fucking quiet.

The night was his domain, his place of work, but he couldn't work with all the noise. He scratched at the spreading whiskers on his chin. *Stop scratching!* his mother would have said.

Shut the hell up, you old bitch!

He was only itching to get back to work.

He left the garage, where he'd silently watched the goings-on and wandered out back to the old shelter. His playmate was quieter now, losing her resolve. It made him smile as he unlocked the combination lock—23-04-39—his dear mother's birthday.

Still, he didn't want the girl to give him the silent treatment. He was going to have to give her a new reason to scream. After all, it was the only noise he had an appreciation for.

The shelter door creaked on its hinges, accompanied by another sound that caught his attention. Laughter, clear and distinct, rose out of the chilly night air, from the direction of the rose garden. Darryl frowned as he scanned the bushes, the thorny branches looking more like the tendrils of a heaving beast made of out shadow.

"Who's there?" He closed the shelter door and locked it.

The laughter arrived again; Darryl recognised a male voice. He retrieved the pen torch from his pocket and shone it on the bushes. If someone was messing around in his mother's garden, he'd snap their fucking neck.

"Get the fuck out of my yard!" He strode across to the lawn, shining the torch back and forth. Out of the corner of his eye, he caught a shape running from the bushes towards the shelter. Darryl swung around the beam of light, but failed to keep pace with the silhouette. "Who the fuck is that? You get off my mother's property or I'll call the cops!"

The shadow laughed; it was a boy's laugh, swirling around him in the air.

"Call the cops," the voice said, "and they'll know your little secret."

Darryl dropped his torch. The beam cast light across a pair of naked feet.

The voice started to laugh again, and trailed along the garage wall and out into the front yard. Darryl experienced a sensation he hadn't felt since his mother died.

Fear.

CHAPTER THIRTEEN

The sound of breaking glass woke Matthew at 3 a.m. He rolled over and rubbed his eyes, trying to see in the dark, but it did little to shift the smog of sleep inside his head. He pulled back the covers and padded to the half-open bedroom door and listened. He saw nothing but the darkened hallway, cold and silent. His parents' door at the end of the hall was closed. He began to question the authenticity of the noise, when he heard it again. A window was being broken downstairs, possibly in the kitchen; someone was breaking in.

Matthew stepped gingerly into the hall, wanting to see, but not wanting to. He glanced up the hall and tried to calculate the distance should he need to run and wake his mother and father. There was another tinkle of glass, followed by the distinct sound of one of the dining chairs scraping on the tiled floor. Matthew jumped and looked to his parents' door again.

Why aren't they rising? Can't they hear this ruckus?

The boy clenched his fists, his fingers were ice-cold. Should he cry out to his father? Or would that only alert the burglar to his presence? Matthew decided it would. His only chance was to make a run for it to his parents' door and wake them before the intruder had any idea he was awake. All he had to do was take a deep breath and run.

The stairs below him creaked, one at first, then another and another.

Shit, he's coming up the stairs!

Matthew froze, his courageous sprint averted before it could even begin. His eyes locked on the top of the staircase and he saw the intruder's shadow slowly rising to the top floor. He told himself to turn and run, to slam his bedroom door, to cry out for Mom or Dad.

"Who… who's there?"

Fear was taking control and his bladder weighed heavy on his insides. The shadow crept closer, its steps heralding its ascension with creak after creak. Matthew took a solitary step backwards and reached for the edge of his bedroom doorway. "Stop…" he said. "I've… I've got a gun."

The shadow reached the final step and stopped. Matthew saw the intruder's hand on the railing.

What sort of burglar doesn't wear gloves?

"You wouldn't shoot your older brother now, would you?"

A sliver of confusion took hold of him.

The figure stepped into the upper hallway and Matthew froze.

"You haven't even got a gun, have you, pussy boy?"

Matthew's mouth and throat were so dry that his voice cracked. "Zac… Zac?"

The figure approached and put an arm around him; he smelled of the earth, and his eyes looked dead. "It's me, pussy boy," Zac said. "It's your big brother."

Matthew tried to slip from the embrace, but was held tight. Everything about Zac was wrong; the way he spoke, and the way he moved, with his back straight and expressive hands. "You're back?" was all he could say.

"Indeed, I am. It's good to see you… pussy boy." Zac chuckled at the term he'd tormented Matthew with so often, but it was as if he was trying it out for the first time. Even stranger was the fact that his breath carried that same earthy smell.

"Did you… did you break in?"

Zac frowned in thought, then smiled anew. "Yes, I did, through the window in the kitchen." He held up his left arm and revealed a long gash from wrist to elbow. It bled profusely. "I may have cut myself."

"Jesus…" Matthew felt a cold sweat break out over his skin.

His brother leaned in close until their noses were almost touching. "You're afraid, aren't you, pussy boy? That's what he calls you, isn't it?"

"Wha… what happened to you?"

Zac's mouth was vile. "Let's go wake Max and Carol."

Max Campbell dreamed he was suffocating. He was splayed out naked on the floor of a strange house, with a plastic funnel taped inside his mouth. Above him, a shadow loomed, about to tip the contents of a gasoline can down his throat.

"Father!"

Max awoke and felt something pressing down on his face. He sat up urgently and pushed the pillow away. He heard crying and laughing in the room, and struggled to discern the three shadows at the end of the bed.

"So glad you could join us," one of the shadows said. It was holding the pillow.

"What the fuck?" Max said.

Slowly the shadows sharpened in the curtain-filtered moonlight.

Carol huddled in the corner of the bedroom with Matthew. The third figure was a boy who looked a lot like—

"Zac?"

Zac's slimy grin shone. "Hello, Daddy."

Max got to his feet, adrenalin rushing from his chest down to his forearms. "You little son of a bitch. Where the fuck have you been?" He took a step toward the end of the bed, eager to get a hold of his son. The boy was going to get a tanning.

"You know, you shouldn't call Mother a bitch," Zac said.

Max didn't like the boy's cockiness, not just his choice of words, but the clipped tone he used. He grabbed the boy by the shirt sleeve. "You shut the hell up and listen to me."

Zac's fist whipped out in an arc and caught Max under the jaw.

The big man staggered back onto the bed. He stared, wide-eyed, but was back on his feet a moment later with his fist raised. "Oh, you're gonna get it now!"

He lashed out, but Zac dodged the blow and brought his fist into Max's nose. The big man felt a sickening crack in the centre of his face, and blood poured into his mouth. A cascade of stars sparkled behind his eyes and dropped him to his knees. Through a haze of pain, he tried to conceive how his son could suddenly fight. Through the ringing in his skull, he heard the boy laughing.

"You really are a worthless excuse for a man!"

Carol couldn't believe the words coming from Zac's lips. She couldn't believe what was happening, that her son had returned and was unleashing brutal punishment upon his father. But he was no longer her boy. The very moment he'd entered the room and pulled her from the bed, she'd known it to be true. She felt her other son's hand pulling on her nightgown, heard his sobs of terror, and when she looked at him, she feared she was about to lose him too.

Zac laughed as he kicked Max in the ribs. She'd never seen Zac hit anyone before, and she'd never seen her husband go down during a fight. She'd never forget how, when they were courting, Max had "valiantly" knocked out another man's front teeth for looking at her during a dinner dance, and now she was terrified of what he'd do to Zac if he ever got to his feet.

"Do you hear me, *father*?" Zac said as he looked down on his father. "You're worthless!" Max's right arm whipped out to grab his son, but Zac was too quick. He skirted away, and then promptly crossed the distance with a running kick to Max's ass. The big man wailed and collapsed onto his side, clutching his groin. Zac looked at Carol, hysterical glee painted on his face. "I've got him crawling on the ground like a worthless dog, Mother. Do you see?" He didn't wait for her to answer. He skipped around Max and kicked him in the face. The wound on his nose split even wider.

Max shrieked and spat blood all over the carpet and bedspread. "I'm gonna kill you!" her husband cried.

Zac let a long ropey trail of spit fall from his mouth, and onto his father's head. "You'll be begging for death soon enough Father, but all I can guarantee is there will be a lot of pain between now and then!"

Matthew squeezed his eyes shut and covered his ears, but it did nothing to block out the sound of Zac beating his father to death.

Yet he was too weak not to look, and Matthew opened his eyes long enough to catch a glimpse of the brutality. Zac was relentless, overcome with violent nonchalance, taking great pride in punching, kicking and spitting on Max, only occasionally stopping to laugh at his handiwork.

His dad was in the foetal position, trying to cover his head and ribs, but Zac's fists and feet managed to find chinks in his father's protection, and extract a new chorus of agony. The carpet resembled a Jackson Pollock painting, but Max's face was Zac's true masterpiece. His brother kicked his father between the legs again and Max let out a gasping shriek. Matthew couldn't take it anymore. Zac had to stop.

As if he'd heard his thoughts, Zac turned and smiled. "I'm only administering the same punishment Max used to impose upon you and Zachary."

Matthew shook his head. "Don't…"

Zac's boot connected with the man's mouth. Max spat out two front teeth. Zac motioned for Matthew to come forward. "Here, take your turn," Zac said. "Give your father what he deserves."

Matthew saw his father's eyes beneath all the blood. They were filled desperate fear. He turned away.

"Zac, stop!" Carol's face shone with tears. She attempted to climb to her knees, but Matthew clutched her nightgown to keep her back.

"Sorry Mother, but Max has to pay his dues!" Zac emphasised his determination by punching Max in the kidneys.

"You're not my son!" Carol said. "You wouldn't do this!"

Zac frowned. "How do you know he wouldn't, hmm? How do you know what goes on inside your boy's head?" He tapped his temple with a bloodied finger. "I know exactly what's in Zac's head, and do you want to know *how* I know? Because I put it there!"

Matthew's brother laughed. It was the hearty laugh of a man—not a boy. His back arched at the exertion. Then he dropped to his knees, in his father's blood, while Max tried to protect his mangled face with trembling hands. "Zac's always wanted to do this. He just didn't know how. Until I came along."

Carol reached for him. "Please stop. You're killing your father."

The boy licked stray flecks of blood from his lips. "Don't worry *Mother*," he said. "I've got plenty of love to share. Once I'm done with Father here—you're next."

CHAPTER FOURTEEN

Ben awoke at dawn and left the house, eager not to make contact with his wife, but more to answer the burning questions about the Kemper House.

The street was eerily quiet, and Ben couldn't help but feel a strange sense of solitude as the sun rose over the hills to the east. He slurped at the coffee from his thermos and dismissed the sensation as lethargy. He'd hardly slept at all, not with Megan's last words to him and the events of the day prior still lingering in his mind.

As he climbed into his car, he stopped and gave the Kemper House another look. The temptation to break in and find the truth was palpable. The police had already had their way with the place, and as far as he was aware, no one had taken ownership of the property. What would be the harm in prying open a window and getting a first-hand look at the house from Hell?

Ben shook his head and started the vehicle. There were safer ways to find out what he wanted to know, and he had quite the list. He needed to speak to Detective Baltzer, not only about the identity of the murdered man, but also about the Cross killings. He needed to discover what the police knew about the Kemper House's evil twin. He reversed out of the driveway and got one last look at the dark edifice on the opposite side of the street.

Who on earth would want to build a house like that?

It didn't matter how many cigarettes Detective Jim Baltzer smoked, nothing would stop the trembling.

He stood in the police station car park as dawn peaked

above the city, and puffed on the cigarette, blue smoke twirling into the air.

The Kemper House case was fading just as quickly.

All he had was a body and the house it was found in.

A vision of the corpse laid out on the autopsy table flashed behind his eyes in tandem with the smell of preserving fluids. Interspersed was a slideshow of another case—crime scene photos of a working girl they had found at the landfill the year before. Together they presented a mingling of fresh and stale death.

He ran a gnarled hand over his lined face and widened his eyes, desperate to find focus. Back inside his office, were photos of a woman's corpse, accompanied by a list of names gracing a whiteboard near the door. The murdered woman and her missing companions. The first victim had been found naked, but wearing evidence of brutal and demeaning torture. The other three women were still missing. The detective had a hunch the man responsible was in his city, but he was no closer to finding him, or the other missing women. The case had dominated his days, until the Kemper House. Baltzer swallowed down his guilt of having to put the former case aside. But he didn't have the luxury of time. He'd have to pull in some of his detectives from the missing women case to start investigating a new, much stranger death.

Sighing, he puffed on the smoke once more, keen to taste something other than decay. He looked across the car park for his car.

That's right, I was going home. The autopsy has been done, so I can go home.

As he walked across the car park, the coroner's laughter still rang in his ears. There was apparently something funny about the fact that he didn't have to make a Y-incision in the corpse, because it had already been done for him.

Baltzer flicked the half-finished cigarette into a pool of rainwater. He fumbled for the keys in his pocket. The way the world staggered around him, he almost felt as if he was intoxicated on too much murder.

"Baltzer?"

The detective turned and looked toward the gate. Immediately, he winced. It was the reporter—Ben fucking Traynor.

"Detective Baltzer, I need to talk to you."

He waved Traynor away and continued toward his car, only to stop.

That's right, I've got a bone to pick with this asshole.

Turning on his heels, he approached the gate.

Traynor immediately started hurling questions at him through the mesh fencing. "Have you identified the victim yet?"

Baltzer pulled the pack of cigarettes from his shirt pocket. "Even if the DNA was complete—which it isn't—and even if we'd notified his next of kin—which we haven't—you'd still have to wait like everyone else."

"So that's a no then. What about the cause of death?"

Baltzer lit his cigarette, careful to take his time. Then he smiled. "Why did you speak to the neighbours before we'd had a chance to interview them?"

Traynor shrugged. "I did my job. Sue me. So, cause of death?"

Baltzer took a long drag on his cigarette. "You know that woman called me to complain? She rang the station because of what you did. Does that seem wrong to you?"

Traynor reached into his pocket and pulled out his Dictaphone. "Detective Baltzer, can you reveal the cause of death of the man found in Willow Street? Are you any closer to catching his killer?"

Baltzer chuckled, smoke chuffing out from his mouth like a train. "You're a piece of fucking work, Traynor."

"Is that your official comment?"

"Okay, here's my official statement." The smug prick was looking to get his teeth kicked in. "The Homicide Department is yet to identify the deceased male located at 72 Willow Street. DNA analysis is expected to be complete in the coming days—"

Traynor pressed the stop button on his Dictaphone. "Wait, what about county records? Bank statements on the house?"

"Yes, we've looked into that. There's no record of anyone having lived in the house for twenty years."

"So who owns it? Is it a government house?"

"We're waiting on the deeds. There are no repayments owing, and it's not listed for sale."

"Is it condemned? Was the guy a squatter?"

"We don't know, alright?" Baltzer threw his cigarette away. "All we know is that the guy cut himself to fucking pieces."

Traynor almost dropped his Dictaphone. "Say again?"

Baltzer chewed his lip, regretting his last words.

"So, are you saying that this was a suicide?"

"Right now we honestly don't know."

"What about the writings on the wall? Could this have been a ritual killing? Could it have been staged? Is this case now taking priority over the murdered prostitutes?"

"Traynor, shut the fuck up, okay? We need more time, and you've just got to lay off. And if you print any of what I just said, I've already warned you about what will happen."

He watched the reporter put the recorder back in his pocket. The frustration on his face looked familiar. Then his eyebrows rose. "Have you looked into who built the house?"

The detective frowned. "No, why?"

"Because I've been told there's another *Kemper House*—identical—right on the other side of town."

As Ben drove over the bridge into northern West Plains, he played back the last moments of his conversation with the detective.

No sooner had Ben mentioned looking into the murders at the other house in 1982, Baltzer's attitude, and patience, had turned sour. He'd declared the insinuations that the crime was ritualistic and connected to a forty-year-old murder case as ludicrous. Worse still, he'd threatened to charge him with obstruction if he continued to hinder the investigation. A second threat to call his editor at *The Gazette* had sent Ben running with his tail between his legs, leaving him no choice but to follow his own investigation. He couldn't get taken off the story now. Not when he was on to something.

He turned left onto Derry Street, the main thoroughfare on the northern side of the city, and drove by a long line of houses with terracotta roofs and neutral facades. The north section of the city was filling up with modern houses, land package estates, their cookie-cutter styles pushing farther into the ranges with each passing year.

With one hand on the steering wheel, he unfolded the printout of old real estate listings for the former Cross residence he'd downloaded on his office computer. Provincial Real Estate had been taking care of the property in the mid-1980s before it was taken off the market, and Ben had a hunch they might still have it on their books. He accessed his cell phone and dialled Provincial's number. A cheery receptionist named Kelly picked up on the third ring.

"Hi Kelly, my name's Ben, and I'd like to inquire about a house on Mayne Avenue, the old gothic style house?"

There was a moment's pause. "I'm sorry sir, but we don't currently have any properties listed for sale on Mayne Avenue."

"Oh, right. It's just, I saw this house and thought, wow, it's a fantastic looking house and when I looked it up I saw that Provincial had been the agency in the past. I wondered if anyone there knew the owner, or—

"I'm sorry sir, but the house isn't on our current listings. Is there another property that you'd like to discuss with us?"

Ben ended the call and slammed his hand down on the steering wheel. He could try the half a dozen other agencies in the city, but he knew he'd be better off getting a closer look at the house itself.

The Mayne Avenue house was identical right down to the leprous paint job and needle spire. Ben sat in his car across the street, in awe of the structure. It was as if the house had somehow uprooted itself from its foundations in Willow Street, and followed him over the bridge.

To Ben this version of the house appeared to be a few years younger than its southern counterpart. The front yard was yellow with drought. Its lone tree grey with death, branches reaching like crooked fingers towards the house. The windows offered no glimpse of the interior, only blackness.

Mayne Avenue was a lot quieter than Ben's neighbourhood. He'd been parked for a few minutes, and no one had ventured by. There was no traffic, not even a taxi, and if Ben wanted to get a closer look, he figured he could do it without being seen. The urge to get inside made his skin itch, so he grabbed his cell, and exited the car.

The street remained clear in both directions, with no sign of watchful neighbours, as Ben approached the Kemper House Mark II. The building appeared to swell in size with each step, the windows peered relentlessly down on him, regardless of the angle, like the gaze of a figure in a painting. The only difference between 1201 Mayne Avenue and 72 Willow Street was the absence of the smell of putrefaction, and for that, Ben was grateful.

He stopped a few yards from the front steps and glanced at the houses next door, careful not to give the impression of being a prowler. Instead, he was a potential buyer, wanting a better look at some potential capital. He took out his phone and took a photo. There was no gate or fence surrounding the house, so Ben was free to walk straight up the path and down the right-hand side. Remnants of grey leaves and branches from the ancient tree crunched beneath his shoes. There were three windows on the ground floor, and two upstairs. An ocular window sat in the wall at the apex of the house. All of the windows were intact, which Ben found odd. He'd thought the house would have made the perfect target for vandals.

The rear yard contained two more dead trees and a rusting swing set, but no other signs that it had ever been inhabited. Together, the house and its grounds looked as if they had been grown from some bad seed rather than built. Ben found it hard to fathom why the Cross family, or the Mortons, hadn't sought to repair the house, or at least repaint it. That's what he would have done. Then again, he wouldn't have given the properties a second look. He admired old houses if they were well-kept and imbued with a sense of charm. But to him, the Kemper Houses were ugly and better off demolished.

He took a deep breath, and climbed the stairs that lead to the back porch. The back door was caked with dust, its hinges barely hanging onto the wood. The brass doorknob had lost its sheen decades ago, probably when the Mortons had closed up and left for good, almost forty years before. He turned the knob and found the door locked. He peered through the door's window, attempting to look inside, but a thick curtain obscured his view.

His reporter's conscience flared, insisting that he only needed to break the glass and reach inside for the lock. But instead he backed away and walked down the steps before the temptation became too much. He left the backyard and walked along the opposite side of the house. Here, it was no different. The entire house was a time capsule, sealed forevermore.

As he passed a window on the lower floor, he caught movement from the corner of his eye. He stopped and looked. A curtain settled back into place as if something or someone had moved it.

It couldn't have been the wind.

There *was* no wind, and even if there was, all the windows were closed, which meant there was a possibility that someone was inside.

He jogged to the front of the house and ascended the steps. He rapped the knocker on the front door, silently begging that it wasn't his imagination or his investigative mind playing tricks. He gave a moment's pause and rapped the knocker again.

"Hello? Is anybody home?"

Ben went to the one of the front windows and tried to peer through, but all he could see was his own desperate reflection. He stepped back to the door. "Sorry to bother you," he said. "I'm from *The Gazette* newspaper and I'd like to talk to you about our new subscription package." He licked his lips impatiently; he was sure he'd seen someone inside. "Hello?"

The front door clicked open and a young boy greeted him, plump-faced, with a bright red woollen jumper and a bowl haircut. Ben could hardly believe his luck.

"Hey, champ." He tried to peak through the gap in the door. "Is your mom or dad home?"

The boy pulled the door wide, and Ben beheld the front living room—and a woman standing at the bottom of the staircase. Her floral print dress was stark against her dark curls and plain complexion.

"Move away from the door," she said.

At first, Ben thought she was speaking to him, until the boy took a few steps back.

"Hey, it's okay," he said offering the woman a kind smile. "This must be your boy."

Her eyes were cold. "We're not interested in whatever it is you're selling."

"You'll have to forgive me," Ben said. "I'm new to this door-to-door sales thing." He looked at the boy, who was regarding him as if he were a stick insect. "It's only my second day. My name's Ben. What's your name, buddy?"

"Don't talk to him," the woman said through gritted teeth and this time she was addressing Ben.

He held out his hands to placate her. "Okay, okay, I'm sorry. I only wanted to speak to the owner of the house." He craned his neck trying to see more of the interior. The woman watched him, but neither she nor the boy moved; in fact, Ben wondered if they'd even blinked. "It's a lovely house—"

"You need to leave."

The woman could have killed him with her eyes alone and the boy seemed as though he would have gladly watched. Ben felt cold air on the front of his body, like he was looking into a refrigerator while his back was warm.

"What's going on?"

A man and a woman appeared from an entryway to the right of the living room. They were in their early fifties and dressed casually, the man with a tie-dye print shirt and jeans, and the woman with a tight-fitting blouse and tan pants. It was the man who'd spoken.

"Hi," Ben said, confused. "I'm from *The Gazette*—"

"He's trespassing," said the woman at the bottom of the stairs.

The newcomers considered her statement and gave Ben a second look. "From *The Gazette* did you say?" the other woman asked.

"That's right. I'm here to offer you a subscription."

"You'd better come in then." Ben thought it strange when she didn't offer a smile with the invitation.

The woman at the stairs beckoned to the boy with a flick of her wrist. He ran to her side and they began to ascend, their eyes upon Ben as he stepped inside.

"You'll have to forgive Cindy," the man said. "She doesn't like uninvited guests."

"Oh, I totally understand," Ben said. "I'm not that fond of salesman either."

"And yet, you're a salesman," the woman said.

"Well, it pays the bills." He quickly changed the subject and took a sweeping look around the living room. "This is a beautiful house. It must be old."

"Ancient," the man said.

The reporter chuckled and offered his hand. "I should introduce myself if I'm going to try and sell you something."

"You told Cindy your name was Ben. Is that not your name?" the woman asked.

The reporter dropped his hand and swallowed. These two were looking at him just like Cindy. "Oh, yeah, of course I did." Again he tried to divert their suspicions. "Sorry, but I didn't catch your names."

"Henry," the man said.

"Belle," said the woman.

"So, Cindy and the boy, are you all related?"

"They're just visiting," Henry said.

"We used to get a lot of visitors coming to look at the house," Belle added quickly.

"Really? I didn't think anyone lived here."

Henry put his hand on Ben's shoulder. "Would you like a tour?"

The deeper Ben was taken into the house, the stranger Henry and Belle became.

The way they walked the hallways, showing him the bedrooms with their matching vintage floral print bedspreads, and speaking in low, droll tones, put Ben on edge. Still, he observed and took mental notes, occasionally chiming in with questions about the house's origins. Another aspect he found odd, was that Cindy and the boy were nowhere to be found. Ben assumed they'd locked themselves away in another bedroom somewhere.

"Do you actually know how old this house is?" Ben asked.

Henry and Belle turned to look at him, their faces expressionless.

Ben smirked and shrugged. "I know you said it was ancient Henry, but looking at it, it must have been built in the early 1900s or something."

"1886," Belle said.

"Who was the builder?"

Henry's lips looked parched. "The Kemper House was built by Eric Kemper."

"He was an immigrant from Prague, right?"

Henry blinked. "The house was built by Eric Kemper in 1886. He was an extremely intelligent man with an eye for detail."

"Was this the only house he built?"

"Mr. Kemper designed and built many others in the city," Belle said. "The old hospital for instance."

Ben scanned the wallpaper and high ceilings. The sunlight barely managed to find its way into the house. "He certainly preferred the dark, didn't he?"

Henry and Belle frowned. It was the first genuine reaction from either of them. Strange that they should react to a remark about someone who'd been dead for more than one hundred and fifty years.

"How long have you two lived here?"

"Oh, a long time," Belle said, and this time she was smiling, but there was no sheen to her teeth.

"I thought this house was unoccupied since the last owners left? The um... the Mortons, they claimed the house was haunted—"

A twinge of recognition hit Ben in the gut as he regarded the couple. Cold sweat prickled at the back of his neck. He swallowed hard, trying not to let his guard down. "Look, I really appreciate the tour, but I'm going to have to get back on down the road." He rifled in his bag and retrieved the day's *Gazette*. He handed it to Henry. "Here's a complimentary edition of the paper. You'll find a number in there for the subscription office, if you're interested."

Henry Morton took the paper, but stood there holding it like he didn't understand its purpose. Belle—Annabelle Morton—put a hand on her husband's shoulder. "Oh, please stay. We'd love for you to see the attic."

Ben backed away, while attempting to calculate how many steps it was to the staircase. His heart had already started running, and he desperately wanted his feet to get the message. The Mortons appeared perplexed, then frustrated, their faces suddenly animated by the prospect of his leaving. He turned to run, and found Mitchell Cross's dead wife Cindy—and her son Nathan—blocking the stairs.

"Where are you going?" Nathan said.

"He's leaving. What do you think he's doing, you stupid boy?" Cindy said through gritted teeth.

Ben held his hands up. "Okay, look, I don't know what the hell is going on here, but I need to go right now."

Cindy's lips trembled with sadness and rage. "You see, Nathan? He's leaving—just like your good for nothing father."

Ben looked down at the boy whose cheeks ran with tears.

"Where are you going?" the boy said.

"You have to let me go..." Ben's heart pounded a drum beat that urged him to flee, to shove the dead boy and his mother aside and run. But how could he push them aside when they shouldn't even be standing before him? They were not real. They couldn't be. He must still be in his car outside, staring at the house. Why would he be stupid enough to go inside? The words of Mitchell Cross, Cindy's tormented husband suddenly rang true.

The house will kill you.

Ben made to run, but a hand gripped his arm. He whirled to see Henry's face, contorted in a silent scream, his mouth so wide that Ben could see darkness at the bottom of his throat. Annabelle stood behind her husband smiling, but her teeth were rotten with decay.

"Come up to the attic," she said. "Come and read his message."

Henry Morton's grip made Ben cry out. He thrashed and railed, but it only brought more pain. His knees gave out from under him. Henry began to drag him back up the hallway. Annabelle clapped her hands like a child about to receive a birthday present. The Cross family, Cindy and Nathan, simply followed them; mournful worshippers on a pilgrimage of retribution.

"You have to let me go!" Ben said as he was pulled along the carpet. "People will look for me! My wife! You have to let me leave!"

Henry trudged on, dragging Ben to the end of the hall. "We could never leave; neither can you."

Belle bent down to look directly into Ben's terrified face. "We tried to leave, but there's no escaping his house."

Henry hefted Ben to his feet. The ungainly man's strength was impossible. "There's no escaping the void once the door is open."

Ben squirmed, but Henry's grip was as strong as steel. "No, please! Stop!" He looked around the room for a weapon, anything. He reached out and grabbed the doorframe, desperate to prevent Henry from moving him any farther. From the corner of his eye he saw Cindy, holding the edge of a kitchen knife to Nathan's throat. The boy sobbed uncontrollably.

Belle reached up to open a hatch in the ceiling. An ornate wooden staircase slid down on a rail to the floor. Ben was dragged up into the attic. He kicked his legs, screaming for someone—anyone—to help him.

"No one is coming," Cindy said from the bottom of the stairs. "Nobody helps those in need."

Nathan swallowed. His tiny Adam's apple pushed against the knife. "There's no sanctuary except the temple."

In the cool of the attic, Ben felt the heat of tears on his face. The room was octagonal and wide. Bare wooden walls were covered in scrawl, painted crudely with fingers dipped in blood. Despite his terror, he made sense of them. He'd seen them before on the walls of the other Kemper House on Willow Street.

Oh, God, the madness is here, too.

Henry dropped Ben hard on the floor and straddled his chest. His wife began lighting the sconces on the walls. The candles came alive at her touch. She started to sing, a lullaby, or hymn, Ben didn't know, but it seemed to drop the temperature in the room by another five degrees.

He slipped his hands free of Henry's grip and swung a punch, hard into his face. It didn't faze the man in the slightest. "Jesus Christ! Help me!"

"There are no gods, but those that reside in the void," Belle said, chastising him.

"And you must not utter the name of a false god in the temple," added Cindy who had ascended the stairs with her little boy, her knife still hovering at his tender neck.

Ben winced as Henry tied a leather strap around his wrists. He stared at all four of them, begging himself to wake up from the nightmare, begging for one last chance to be with his wife. "You're all dead. None of you should be here."

"You're right," Henry said. "We are trapped unless we make an offering, as Eric Kemper did, in order to ascend."

Cindy withdrew the knife from her son's throat and handed it to Belle, who passed it to her husband.

"No!" Ben cried.

The air went still, while above them, at the point where the spire met the apex of the attic roof, a chasm opened. The entire attic became translucent, like water, and beyond lay a night sky comprised of a billion stars. The view rushed forward, traversing millions of light years in an instant, and focused on the darkness between the constellations.

"The endless black," Henry said, as he raised the knife. "Listen to their voices!"

Ben's ears rang. They filled with a burst of white noise. The noise became voices; songs and shouts and utterances, one on top of the other. A babble of indecipherable words from the end of time. It was so loud that Ben wished Henry would plunge the knife into his chest just to end it.

Amidst the cacophony he heard Megan's voice; words of devotion she'd uttered to him on a lone stretch of beach fifteen years before—and the connection was broken.

Ben snapped out of his reverie and grabbed Henry's hands. He shifted his weight and toppled the old man over, but still he refused to release the knife. Ben felt Belle on his back. She clawed at his head and pulled his hair. The reporter lashed out and pushed her away. She slammed against the wall. One of the candles fell and landed in her hair, igniting it with a spark of flame. With an audible whoosh, coils of fire engulfed her body.

"Annabelle!" Henry shoved Ben aside as if he were a doll.

Ben watched as the man went to his wife's aid, only to be swallowed by the same column of flame. Cindy and her son cowered together, screaming as their flaming companions thrashed about the room. The great tongue of fire swept up everything in its path, the dry wood of the attic was the perfect fuel. Ben got to his feet and ran for the stairs. He threw himself down the steps, with the heat of the fire on his back.

CHAPTER FIFTEEN

When Detective Baltzer arrived on the scene at 1201 Mayne Avenue, the dwelling was completely ablaze. Firemen ran in all directions, securing hoses and dousing the house with water, but the veteran detective could see the building was already destroyed. From the other side of the street, where neighbours looked on, he could feel the heat. A great cloud of grey smoke spewed into the air, so thick it made him want to spit.

Nearby, he saw the reporter, Traynor, sitting in the back of an ambulance, gasping for breath. He looked at the fire and the soot on Ben Traynor's face. "You were in that house, weren't you?"

Baltzer's remark widened Ben's eyes, and the mask over his face filled over and over with condensation.

"We have to take him to hospital," one of the paramedics said.

"Give us a minute." Baltzer crouched down to get in Ben's face. "What the fuck were you doing in that house?"

The sheer panic on the reporter's face said it all, but Baltzer saw something else beneath the veneer of sweat and smoke, something in his eyes.

"It was... Mitchell Cross'... house." Ben wheezed.

Baltzer frowned and looked at the house, just as a large section of the roof caved in. Thousands of embers filled the air, sending the firefighters into a frenzy. The detective remembered Ben mentioning the name Cross, back at the station. "Is this about the Willow Street case?"

Traynor nodded, his breathing becoming shallow.

"Didn't I tell you to leave it alone?" Baltzer said. "What the fuck happened? Did you torch the place to get another fucking front page?" He watched Traynor shake his head.

"They…. were… still in… the house."

Baltzer gritted his teeth and reached out to shake Ben's singed coat. "Who, goddamn it?"

"Cross' wife… and… son."

The reporter fell backwards.

The paramedics grabbed him by the arms and laid him down on a stretcher. One of them pushed Baltzer aside to close the doors of the ambulance. "We need to get him to the hospital, now."

"You should be taking him to the fucking psych ward."

The paramedic slammed the doors, and the ambulance pulled away in a hail of sirens and lights. Baltzer's thoughts were as thick as the smoke surrounding Mayne Avenue. He didn't know if Traynor had committed arson, but something had scared the life out of him, and after seeing the sights of the other Kemper House in Willow Street, the detective wondered if it was time to start believing in the impossible.

The Cowley girl's face seemed to be etched permanently on Megan Traynor's vision.

In the quiet loneliness of her house, the events of the girl's death played over and over in Megan's mind, pushing the torturous thoughts of her husband's neglect aside. Her living room was beginning to look like the Cowley's, and when she stared at the carpet, it was if she saw Amy lying there, motionless, her eyes cold. Why a girl of fourteen would choose to take her own life, Megan had no clue.

She was just a child, innocent and naïve. To do such a thing to her mother, to put her through such hell. How could she?

Megan bit her bottom lip. She was being insensitive. Who was she to judge when she didn't know what it was like to have a child of her own? Sadness swelled inside, and she was drawn back to how empty she felt, in love, in life. She shook her head in a bid to shake off these thoughts, but she knew it wouldn't be enough.

She broke into a flurry of exertion, vacuuming the living

room, as if she could remove the girl's ghost from the floor, then pulling out the treadmill. Cold sweat oozed from her skin, as she ran mile after mile, attempting to cleanse her thoughts. She watched the electronic counter tick over, anything to avoid the sadness she felt for the Cowley family, the murdered man in the house across the street, the resentment towards Ben. Tears flooded into the sweat on her cheeks and she squeezed her eyes shut, only opening them when it began to hurt too much.

She glanced out the window into the back yard, and saw another face staring back at her.

It was a man, who immediately ducked out of view as soon as she'd seen him. Megan turned off the treadmill and stopped running. Now, fear fuelled the beating of her heart. It was definitely a man she'd seen, bald with old fashioned glasses.

Gingerly, Megan stepped to the window, and seeing no one she ran to the back door and then the front, locking them both, the image of the dead Cowley girl now superseded by a peeping tom, a new torment for her to bear.

The fact she was alone gripped her like the cold. Instinct told her to call Ben, to get him to come and make her feel safe, but she didn't want that anymore. Instead she found her cell phone on the kitchen bench and began to call 9-1-1.

The phone rang in her hand before she could make the call. She let out a scream.

"H-hello?"

"Is this Mrs. Traynor?"

"Yes, who is this?"

"This is Sergeant McKinney at West Plains 2nd Precinct. I'm calling about your husband."

Megan's mouth turned dry. "Is he okay?"

"He's at the hospital Mrs. Traynor. There was a fire and he suffered smoke inhalation."

"Oh, my God."

"We just wanted to inform you ma'am. You should probably head over there."

Megan ended the call and ran for the door.

Ben floated in the void, between the world of the living and the dead. All he could see was darkness, while the inside of his skull rang with a chorus of screams.

Although blind, he sensed that he was moving forward, a satellite of flesh soaring toward doom. As he ascended, the screams increased in intensity, pressing through the skin of his head, reverberating through the bone. His brain frantically sought to block out the cries, but it couldn't shake the need to understand. The screams weren't screams at all, but rather a single chain of words chanted over and over.

When he thought the darkness would finally claim his sanity, Ben saw a spark of light and willed himself toward it. The light swelled as Ben travelled millions of miles with each beat of his heart, and he hoped it was the proverbial tunnel, described by so many who'd crossed over and returned. If he was going to die, he wanted to die in the light.

The light was not from a star, but a shifting mass. Ben cried out at the sight of it, a behemoth made from billions and billions of writhing shapes. He wanted to turn his head or cover his eyes, but he was frozen in the void and the gigantic shape drew him in like a magnet.

The mass of contorted light was a construction of human souls, trapped and twisted to become the torso and limbs of a colossal creature. Ben's soul raced towards it, faster and faster. The thing opened its mouth to accept him, while human souls toppled from its jaws, falling through space only to be caught in its impossible hands and re-devoured.

It reached out to pluck Ben from nowhere. He looked down at its man-made flesh and felt thousands of hands pulling on him, begging him to become one with them. And when he looked up at the creature's ever-shifting face, its eyes were windows and its mouth was a door—the door to the Kemper House.

Ben awoke to the taste of smoke on his tongue and terror in his heart. He sat up in bed and tried to disconnect himself from the nightmare. His surroundings were alien, the wide room with multiple beds not making any sense, even his breathing was unnatural. Feeling suffocated, he reached up and pulled the oxygen mask from his face. He felt cold fingertips on his arm and cried out.

"Ben, Ben, it's okay." His wife squeezed his arm. "You're in the hospital."

"Megan?"

His view of the other hospital beds sharpened. The ping of a heart rate monitor made him jump.

"Calm down," Megan said. "You're making yourself anxious."

The events at Mayne Avenue rushed into his head: the ghosts of the Mortons and the Crosses trying to murder him. He wanted to tell his wife what happened, hell, he wanted to tell everyone, but he doubted anyone would think him sane once he did. Ben took a long breath and concentrated on his wife's face. She appeared genuinely worried. "I... I'm glad you're here," he said.

Megan took a half-step back from the bed. "I didn't know what to think when the police called," she said, sitting down in a nearby chair. "What were you doing at that house?"

Ben laid his head back on the pillows. "It wasn't just any house. It was the same house as the one we live across the road from."

Megan raised an eyebrow. "What are you talking about?"

"The house across the street where that man was murdered. There's another one, identical, in Mayne Avenue, built by the same architect."

"So? Houses are built by the plan all the time."

"Not more than a hundred and fifty years ago they weren't. Don't you think it's odd, that two identical houses were built by the same man, on the opposite sides of town?"

Megan sighed. "Maybe the guy who built it was really rich and wanted to live on the other side of town as well?"

Ben sat up. He felt strength returning to his body. "I went to the house on Mayne Avenue because other people had died there. A woman murdered her son in the house during the 1970s, and another couple reported strange occurrences a decade later."

Megan rubbed her palms on her jeans and stood as if to leave. "Ben..."

"You can't even be in the same room with me anymore, can you?"

His wife turned. "You should hear yourself."

"The woman who killed her son, Cindy Cross, she tried to kill her husband, too. He came to *The Gazette* to warn me about the house on Willow Street. There's something... wrong... with that house." He took another long breath. "There was *definitely* something wrong with the house in Mayne Avenue."

Megan sat back down. "What happened at that place? How did the fire start?"

He avoided her gaze. "I... I went to Mayne Avenue to see if I could get some idea of what happened in the Willow Street house. I mean, the houses were identical. I'm ashamed to admit that I broke in—"

"Jesus!" Megan said.

"—I climbed into the attic. There were candles. I lit one and dropped the damn thing on some old linen. The flames spread so quickly I couldn't stop them."

Megan put her head in her hands. "What were you thinking? What if the owners decide to sue you, sue us? What if the cops decide to charge you?"

Ben swallowed. He couldn't believe how convincing a liar he'd become. "No one has lived in that house for decades. As for the cops, well, I'll cross that bridge if it comes to that."

He saw tears in his wife's eyes. "I can't do this anymore," she said. "You're obsessed with this. Why can't you just leave the detective work to the police?"

"Because this is happening on our doorstep. And I won't feel safe until I know what happened in that house."

Megan threw up her hands in frustration. "You're not a crusader, fighting for people's rights! You're just a reporter. Somebody died in a house, and honestly no one cares about it but you!"

Ben scowled. "That's bullshit—"

"The girl who killed herself in the house up the road—that's more important!"

"Maybe the two things are connected."

"How could they possibly be connected? Just listen to yourself!"

The arrival of a nurse in the room brought their argument to a halt. The broad-shouldered woman gave them a foul stare. "You need to keep the noise down in here," she said. "This is a hospital." She left them without another word.

Megan nodded and scooped up her handbag. "You're right. I'm very sorry. I was just leaving."

"Megan wait—"

She stopped, but didn't turn to face him. He saw she was trembling.

"No, I'm leaving," she said. "I'm leaving *you*." She fished a set of keys from inside her jeans pocket and placed them on the tray table. "I've left your car outside."

Ben pulled himself off the bed, her words leaving him more breathless than the smoke. "Wait… what do you mean, you're leaving?"

"There's more to life than secrets and lies," his wife said. "Life is what's right in front of you."

"Megan…"

"I'm going back to the house to collect my things, and I'm leaving. Don't try to follow me."

She left before he could say another word, and as much as it pained him, he felt relieved that she'd be away from the Kemper House's reach.

After Megan had gone, he rose and wandered the halls of the hospital. The general ward on the third floor, where Ben had been admitted, was relatively new, but the lower floors were part of the original building. He became mesmerised by the varnished wood panelling, and the ornate cream-coloured ceilings. And it was as he admired the centuries-old architecture that the words of Annabelle Morton's ghost came to him.

Mr. Kemper designed and built many buildings…the old hospital, for instance.

Ben looked over his shoulder, suddenly finding the decor threatening. Or was he just imagining it? He sat on one of the chairs outside the clinic, and tried to catch his breath. Had he conjured the ghosts of Cindy and Nathan and the Mortons to suit his theories about the Kemper House? What if Megan was right, that he was obsessed? He ran a hand through his hair, frantically trying to convince himself the lie he'd told his wife hadn't really happened

Fuck—did I burn down the house?

This particular area was empty of patients, but the voices of the nurses and the administration staff carried up the hall. Ben was thankful to hear them, to feel some connection with reality. He stood, deciding to return to his room, when he saw a plaque on the wall. Its marble surface shone in the fluorescent light.

WEST PLAINS GENERAL HOSPITAL
Constructed 1888
Officially opened by: Governor William. F. Lloyd
December 7, 1889
Architect: E.B. Kemper

The etched words mocked him. Thin red veins in the marble pulsed with impossible blood, of all the people who had been born—and had died—inside the walls of the hospital. His gut roiled in synch with his mind as it conjured the dream he'd had of the behemoth in the darkness of space. So many souls sacrificed.

Ben had to get away; from the hospital, from Willow Street— and the town.

He turned to run for the elevator, when the elevator doors opened and a familiar face greeted him—Mitchell Cross. The man's blanched visage trembled with an inner rage. His eyes were bloodshot from prolonged mourning. He held a length of steel pipe in his hand. When he spoke, his breath smelled like he was rotting on the inside. "I told you not to go in that house."

CHAPTER SIXTEEN

His coffee was cold and stale, but Detective Baltzer swallowed it down in the hope it would help his mind make sense of the mess that was Willow Street.

The crime scene photographs from the Kemper House were spread out on his desk and wall, a pastiche of the house's filthy walls covered in filthy words and the impossible body, blooming like a corpse flower in all its glory.

Baltzer had read and re-read the autopsy report, and even though it spelled out exactly what the man had done to himself, it still didn't explain why. The coroner was certain the wounds, including the evisceration of the chest cavity, had been done by the victim. There was no other DNA in the house; no fingerprints, and no blood but the victim's. It was a suicide, and one of the strangest Baltzer, and the coroner had ever seen.

The detective shifted his gaze away from the autopsy report to the photographs of the foreign words that had been written on the walls in the Kemper House. They had been found everywhere: in the kitchen, behind the refrigerator, in the hall behind a mirror, and even behind the bathroom door. Baltzer was awaiting the full translations, but early investigations indicated that the suicide was indeed occult in nature.

Christ, one only had to look at the body and the knife to see that.

He thought about calling on the FBI, but he didn't want those fuckers taking all the glory, and he didn't need them stepping all over his investigations. Which brought him to Ben Traynor. The man was becoming a pain in his ass, running his own investigation for *The Gazette*. He didn't believe Traynor's story about the fire at Mayne Avenue one iota, and he was tempted to go to the hospital and charge him with obstruction, just to get him out of his way.

He'd already looked into the Cross case. The mother and child were dead and the house hadn't been lived in for decades. The ridiculous notions that they were still living there, told him the reporter was either crazy—or hiding something. Baltzer's gut told him it was more than likely both.

Still, he had to admit, the fact there was a second Kemper House was odd. To build a house in the late 19th century you needed to be in the money, and to build two within a year meant you needed to be the wealthiest man in town, or aligned with one. Baltzer had looked into Eric Kemper's history and all indications said he was a nobody, a poor emigrant from Prague, looking for a new start in the Land of the Free. Kemper had never married or had any children. The guy had nothing but the shirt on his back. Somewhere along the line, he became influential enough to build two houses and two hospitals in the city. Historical records were less than useful, revealing details of Kemper's exploits, only after he became the city's top architect. Baltzer could see the immigrant forged a strong connection influence to Mayor William Lloyd and in a very short space of time.

He pushed the accumulated data to one side of his desk, eager to get away from it. He got up from his desk and grabbed his coat, ready to call it a night, when Dr. Carl Brandt, one of the coroner's forensic specialists, knocked on his door. The tall, thin technician seemed jittery, bobbing on his heels.

"You got a minute, Detective?"

"I was about to punch my card."

"Oh, you're going to want to hear this." Brandt produced the evidence bag containing the knife the victim had used to carve himself up. "The analysis on the knife came back and it's really fascinating."

Baltzer shrugged on his coat. "Well, unless it spoke to you, and told you why it carved open that guy like a Christmas fucking ham, it can wait until tomorrow."

Brandt smirked, and pointed to the symbols that had been etched into the steel. "We're still trying to determine what these symbols mean. Actually, we're still not certain it's a language at all—but what the knife is made out of, is even more interesting."

"Stainless steel is it?" Baltzer sighed.

"No, well, yes, it's definitely steel, but it's been mixed with other alloys. There's some gold and bronze in here. We've got some of the experts at the university to take a look at it and they told us that this knife is really old."

Baltzer chewed his lip as thoughts of Eric Kemper came to mind. "Like hundreds of years old?"

Brandt shook his head. "No, no, no. They think it could be thousands of years old. This could actually have been made during the Bronze Age."

Baltzer stared at the knife enclosed in the plastic evidence bag. The blade was dull, grey, and etched with gold symbols. The metal handle had lost its sheen, but it was still just a knife.

"So this guy didn't just grab the first one out of the woodblock then?"

"No, the experts at the university said it could be an athame—a sacrificial knife. They wanted to do some carbon testing on it, to see how old it actually is, but naturally, it's evidence, so I couldn't let them do that—"

"Okay, okay, so the knife is very old. A lot of the stuff in that house was old. Maybe the victim was a collector."

"Maybe..." The specialist held up the knife to the light. "But why kill yourself with this? When as you said, he could have used any of the kitchen knives. And why write those phrases on the wall? I think he *meant* to kill himself with this."

Baltzer took the knife from Brandt and scratched his jaw in frustration. "If you ask me, he was just a psycho, whose name we don't even know." He stared Brandt down. "Are you any closer to finding out who this guy was?"

"Well, he's not in any of our records. His fingerprints and dental scans came up with nada, and as you know, the house has been unoccupied for years."

"Yeah, yeah great. He's a goddamn nobody. Are you sure there's nothing at all about him that could help us identify him?"

Brandt opened the folder he was carrying along with the knife. "The amount of mutilation made it hard to find any distinguishing marks, and he had no broken bones."

"How old was this guy?"

"Hard to say exactly, but sutures in the skull indicate he was somewhere between fifty and sixty years old at the time of his death. His blood type was AB positive, which is not uncommon, but actually there was something about his blood tests that intrigues me."

Baltzer raised his eyebrows. "How so?"

Brandt scratched at his scruffy hair. "Well, this guy had antigens in his blood for the bubonic plague."

Baltzer frowned. "Isn't that an ancient disease?"

"It's still around in some parts of the world, but it's very strange that this man had it and survived. It's possible that he picked it up overseas and received treatment."

"Can you find out?"

"We can try, but it could take a while."

Baltzer sighed. "I've waited this long."

Brandt turned to leave. "Well, goodnight, Detective."

Baltzer tried to fathom the new information the forensic specialist had given him. His office was about to overflow with clues, and here was another layer to the puzzle with no answer in sight. The case was so complex and overwhelming that he was inclined to let it gather dust in the filing cabinets, but the bizarre nature of the death—and the house—was like a shard of glass under his skin. He looked down at the knife in the evidence bag and tried to imagine the man cutting into his own skin. Baltzer picked up the knife and felt its heft in his palm. It was heavy, but its weight was evenly distributed.

"Too heavy to be a throwing dagger," he said out loud.

He ran a thumb over the etchings in the blade. He could see flecks of dark material against the muted gold, the victim's dried blood in every nook and cranny. He put the knife down on the table, suddenly keen to forget it and go home. He moved to turn off the light switch, and was giving the photographs of the hand written scrawl one last look when he had a thought.

He approached the display on the wall, specifically the photo of handwriting found in the Kemper House's kitchen. He retrieved the knife from the table and held it up to the light.

The symbol on the tip of the blade matched a similar scrawl on the wall above the kitchen sink, and beneath the symbol was a crudely written word.

"Doosh?" Baltzer said. "No, *Duch*." The knife hummed in his hand. Startled, the detective almost dropped the blade. "What the fuck was that?"

Had it hummed? He wasn't sure, but the knife had taken on an allure that he felt drawn to.

"Duch," he said again. The knife resonated like a tuning fork in his grip. "Fuck!" This time, the knife clattered to the floor.

Baltzer glanced around his office and then out into the darkened squad room. He was completely alone, the only witness to whatever had just happened. He bent to retrieve the knife, when he realised it was already in his hand. He exclaimed and dropped it a second time. His mind told him to run.

The room was closing in. The photographs of the scene were now as large as paintings on an art gallery wall. Baltzer threw the knife on his desk, and started pulling the photos off the wall in a frenzy. They fluttered to the floor like dead leaves. His head pounded, and his vision blurred. The back of his throat tasted like metal. He swayed as he crouched to pick up the evidence. He thought he would pass out.

Am I having a heart attack?

He clutched his chest, but there was no spreading pain, no nausea. The sensations he felt went much deeper, a tight coil unravelling inside his head. He didn't know if he was dying, but the heady confusion he experienced made him wish he was. He dropped a handful of photos into the evidence box and in doing so, uncovered the knife he'd left on the desk. There was fresh blood on its edge.

He picked up the knife and his palm flared with a stinging pain. The blood had come from his palm—a long red slash from wrist to index finger. The detective had no idea how it had happened. Had he inadvertently cut himself picking it up, or had he traced the oozing path on purpose?

"I have to get out of here," he said.

Baltzer held the knife up and gazed longingly at its gleam. His tongue also defied him. *"Davam ti sve dusi,"* he said. Panic seized his heart as his head translated the foreign words he'd spoken.

I give you my soul.

Before he could conjure the reasons for saying such a phrase, Baltzer drew the blade down the inside of his arm. He cried out for someone to come and save him, but all that answered was his blood. It ran snake-like. It pooled inside his elbow and then fell. When the seventh drop kissed the floor, the air in front of Baltzer's terrified eyes opened a window into a hidden landscape.

Gazing through the flickering portal, the detective saw a night sky full of stars. He gasped and dropped to his knees as the view shifted around and down to provide a bird's eye view of the city. He knew it was his city because he'd seen it many times from the air. Baltzer's vision soared down and over the cityscape, twisting and turning. He screamed as his viewpoint defied gravity while his body remained frozen. The thrum of his pulse let the blood flow, adding more fuel to the spell.

He attempted to drop the knife but the hilt was stuck fast by his congealed blood. His soul was rooted to the spot, his gaze locked on the ground below. The floor of the world rushed up to meet him, taking him to a street he knew all too well. The dark house sat on the corner, a central point on a black map lined and veined with souls. But the knife did not take him there; instead it drew him to the house next door. He passed through the roof as if it was water. He could see every room and every hall.

His journey came to its end in the master bedroom, where he saw a man and woman, both dead, and two boys, their eyes locked on one another. The boy standing dominant over the other, turned to address the detective.

"Give me the knife." the boy said.

The flesh of Baltzer's palm ripped as the knife threw itself through the gap in reality. The boy caught it, and sneered.

"Much obliged Detective. Sadly, you're no longer needed."

The gap snapped shut. Baltzer's psyche shattered, the force of it driving the detective against the wall. He slumped to the floor, and all thoughts and memories of what he'd seen and who he was, pooled onto the floor around him.

CHAPTER SEVENTEEN

When Matthew Campbell saw the hole open up inside his parents' bedroom, and his brother pluck a knife from the other side before closing the fissure with a flick of his wrist, he truly believed Zachary had been subsumed by an impossible force, and was being used to destroy, not only his family, but everyone in the street, and maybe the world.

The way the boy moved, how he stared longingly at the strange weapon in his hand, there was no doubt in Matthew's mind that Zac was no longer in control. Matthew Campbell looked at his mother's and father's corpses, and realised he would be next. Yet, he wouldn't run, not until he was certain his brother couldn't be saved.

"What have you done with my brother?" His voice caused Zac to raise his head from the knife.

"Oh, hello pussy boy," Zac said. "I forgot you were there." He stood over the body of Max and Carol, grinning.

Matthew clenched his fists. The room smelled of his parents' blood. He wanted to retch, but told himself to stay focused "Stop using his voice. I know you're not my brother."

Zac tilted his head like a curious mutt. "You do, do you?"

"You opened a portal and took that knife from the other side. My brother couldn't even open a jar of pickles on his own. So yeah, I know you're not my brother."

Zac's smile grew impossibly wider. "You're smarter than you look. But soon you'll be as dead as Max and Carol here."

Matthew saw the glassiness of his parents' unblinking eyes and silently begged their forgiveness.

"Who are you, really?" Matthew said. "What do you want?"

Zac popped out his bottom lip. "Oh, maybe you're not so

smart? I thought you knew—I'm from the house next door."

Matthew bit his tongue to stifle a gasp. "The Kemper House?"

"The one and the same," Zac said. "I've literally been dying to get out of there for a while, now." Zac shook his arms, shivering the muscles beneath the skin. "It feels good to be free."

"But no one lives in that house."

Zac bent down to Max Campbell's dead body and poked the tip of the knife in between his father's lips. Matthew felt his own skin go cold as the creature who looked like his brother slid the blade inside, the steel clacking against Max's teeth.

"Wha... what are you doing?"

Zac looked up as he worked. "Whatever I want."

Matthew swallowed. "Please... stop. Don't!"

Zac turned his wrist and there was a slick tearing of flesh. Dark, dead blood drooled from Max's mouth and seeped into the carpet.

Matthew wanted to close his eyes and scream, but he was hypnotised. The boy pulled the knife free and pushed his fingers into the open mouth.

"Stop!" Matthew cried.

Zac's face became a scowl. "Do not impose your weakness upon me!" His brother's bellow sent a jolt through Matthew's body. "This is my time. My reckoning. His will!" Before Matthew could utter another word, Zac wrenched his hand from Max's mouth, and a long chunk of flesh came with it. He dangled a blood-soaked length of meat in front of Matthew's face like a prize fish. Matthew's eyes took in every glistening contour of the tissue, his brain identifying it as a tongue—his father's tongue.

"You do not speak to me in that way," Zac said. "No one speaks to me in that way. No one but the one I worship!"

Blood from the tongue trailed a path down Zac's arm. Matthew couldn't look away, no matter how much he wanted to.

"This is where Max's power came from," Zac said. He considered the appendage with a lascivious smile. "Every day of your life he belittled you, insulted you, even spat at you." He pressed closer and Matthew turned a cheek. "I have taken away his power. The dark God I love has made it so. Here, see what I have reduced your tormentor to."

Matthew shook his head.

"Take it!"

"No!"

Zac laughed, a long chuckle that rose from deep within the other soul inside him; the soul that found unbridled satisfaction in cutting grown men to pieces in the name of an unseen god. He tossed the tongue on top of Max's lifeless form. The piece of muscle rolled onto the floor like a worm. Zac cut his laughing short and about-faced to point the knife at Matthew. "You didn't know I was there, because I made sure you didn't. But I saw you and your mommy and daddy and your stupid brother and all the other specks of shit living on the street. I've been watching since before you were born—before all of you were born. So many have lived and died, in this street, in this world and I've seen it all."

Matthew blinked, partly trying to understand what Zac was saying, but also to free his mind of the foul acts his brother was committing. It was pointless because Matthew couldn't disconnect Zac from whatever it was that was talking through him.

"I can see the cogs turning in your mind," Zac said. "I used to be like you—oblivious. And then I opened my eyes." He waved the knife dismissively. "Anyway, that was the old me. This," he took a deep breath, "is the almost new me."

Beads of sweat fell from Matthew's head to the rug. "So, what, you're a ghost?"

Zac chuckled. "You want to know what I am—fine." He waved his knife at Max and Carol. "You're going to end up like these two, anyway."

Terror settled in Matthew's gut, but he tried not to let it show and concentrated on thoughts of escape as Zac paraded around the bodies.

"This is just one stage of a process… a rebirth."

"But, why?" Matthew imagined that his brother would suddenly burst open like an egg sac, and larvae would emerge.

"It is my purpose. It is His gift to me. He chose me to do his will." He pointed his knife at Matthew once more. "I have to hurry and ready His house."

Matthew tensed, ready for the inevitable attack, but for once in his life he had to take a stand—if not for himself—for his brother. He looked at Zac's sneering vile expression and tried to remember how his brother used to be, cocky and full of bravado.

Matthew thought back to the times when they were little, before hormones kicked in and their father made everything a competition. The times when they were having fun just growing up, being brothers. He summoned those thoughts and rose to his feet as Zac approached, knife pointing in his direction.

"Now stay still, pussy boy."

Matthew darted to the left as the blade came down in a savage arc. It missed him by inches. Zac's mouth opened in surprise, but only for a moment as the demonic grin took hold again, the creature inside clearly enjoying the sport.

"Well, this is new," Zac said. "Your brother told me you were weak."

"You might look like Zac, but you're nothing like him on the inside." Matthew clenched his fists and gazed upon his dead mother and father. Despite their differences, they were still his parents, and if his stupid father had drummed anything into him, it was never to back down from a fight. "If you want to kill me, you'll have to work for it."

Zac flipped the knife from his right hand, to his left, and back again. "Is that so?" Then he shrugged. "You're not the first to threaten me, to try and subvert my cause," He pounded his hand against his chest. "I am protected!"

Matthew watched a trail of spittle run from Zac's lips. The thing inside his brother was enraged with insanity. Matthew took a deep breath for courage and circled his brother, edged closer to the bedroom door. If he could get to it, he could make a run for it, out of the house and out into the street where he could yell for help.

Zac lunged.

Matthew moved to the left to dodge the blade, but in avoiding Zac he rolled his left ankle and fell to the floor. A shard of pain spiked up his leg. He quickly got to his feet, before Zac had the chance to get on top of him.

"There's no avoiding this." Zac swiped the knife across the air, making it sing. "You're going to feel this in your flesh, and I'm going to feel the warmth of your blood on my hands."

Matthew put his back to the wall and kept his eye on the knife.

Zac drew its edge across his own palm and then lapped at the blood with a greedy tongue.

Matthew fought the urge to vomit.

"You know I don't even need this," Zac said. "I could just snuff you out like I did your brother when he crawled inside my coffin."

Matthew swallowed, as he thought of his brother suffering at this creature's hands.

The house is bait, and once the hook goes in…" He pushed the tip of the knife right through his palm and out the other side. Fresh blood mixed with old on the floor. "I get your body. He gets your soul."

While Zac's mannerisms continued to shift into darker territory, Matthew struggled to understand who—or what— was threatening him. Going by the fact it could inflict injury on itself and feel no pain, it must have been an alien creature or a ghost; an entity with human traits, but definitely not a child. This was a man—and a crazy one.

"Why did you have to kill my brother?" Matthew's chest heaved with tempered rage.

"The old man I used to be was getting stale," Zac said. "And once I'm done with Zac, I'll move on to the next body, and the next, until I find the right one. Zac's simply a means to an end." He pointed the knife at his parents' corpses. "Just like Mommy and Daddy, here."

"Shut up!" Matthew said.

"Make me, pussy boy. Come on."

Matthew dug his heels into the carpet. But before he could move, Zac launched himself over the bed, bounded off the springs and landed directly in front of the bedroom door. His smile oozed with spit.

"You think I don't know what you're planning? I know every path you could possibly take. I've walked them all. He has shown me all the paths that could possibly be."

Matthew had no choice, he had to run or die trying. He clenched his hands into fists, and took a deep breath. "You always treated me like shit, Zac, you know that?"

"Why are you talking to him? He's dead."

Matthew ignored the creature and spoke directly to his brother. "You called me pussy boy all my life. You taunted me, you hit me, and you were always Mom's favourite."

Zac picked at his fingernails with the tip of the blade. "You're wasting your breath. Your brother's dead. I took his soul and buried it at the end of time and the darkness ate him up and shat him out like he was nothing."

Matthew gritted his teeth. "But I still loved you." He feigned sadness and was grateful that genuine tears of terror ran down his cheeks, adding to the performance. He watched Zac lower his knife arm. He ran at his brother, crossing the space between them with two steps.

Zac's inhabitant was caught off guard, and was too slow to raise the knife and block his fist. Zac's nose broke beneath Matthew's knuckles and Matthew laughed as his brother fell back on his ass.

"That's for all those times you punched me, you asshole!"

Matthew ran for the door, his hand reaching for the handle, when a stinging pain jolted across the back of his right leg. He toppled into the door and looked up to see his brother licking blood from the edge of his knife.

"You taste good!" Zac said as he stood.

Matthew scrambled to his knees, ignoring the open wound in his calf, and gripped the handle to wrench the door open. He looked over his shoulder to see Zac stabbing wildly, using the knife as leverage to pursue him.

"I'm going to cut you into a hundred pieces, pussy boy!"

Matthew opened the door and crawled along the floor, his calf screaming with each movement. He knew by the spreading warmth that the cut was deep, but he had to get to his feet. He lifted his good leg but came down hard. His right leg was useless.

"Look at you," Zac said, standing over him. "A pussy boy to the very end."

Matthew's bloody leg sent sparks of agony through his entire body. His fingers, slick with sweat, found little purchase on the polished wood floor as he struggled to focus, dragging himself inch-by-inch towards the stairs.

Zac laughed. "If you can get to your feet, I might let you live."

Matthew pressed his face into the floor, willing himself to rise, to defy his brother and the thing inside him. His leg was numb and cold, which he was grateful for, but he could also feel the cold spreading through the rest of his body. He was losing too much blood. He pulled his legs beneath him. The cut burned as it stretched, but Matthew clenched his teeth and pushed on.

"That's it pussy boy." Zac crouched beside him. "Make a run for it. The back door is just down those stairs."

"Fuck you!" Matthew spat, but his brother only laughed.

"That's the spirit," Zac pulled Matthew to his feet.

"Don't fucking touch me!" He swayed, and the hall swayed with him. Black spots burst behind his eyes.

"Run, pussy boy! Run!"

Matthew put all his weight on his good leg and skipped down the hall. His brother's laughter taunted him with each pointless step. His body wanted him to give in, to fall to the floor and just die, but his mind screamed no.

"Here, let me help you!" Zac grabbed Matthew by the arm.

With the last of his strength, Matthew whipped his right fist around to catch Zac's jaw, but his brother was simply too fast. He blocked the blow and twisted Matthew's arm hard behind his back. Matthew arced beneath the fresh wave of pain.

"I was trying to help you, pussy boy!" Zac shoved him forward. The stairs came rushing up to meet him. He put his hands out to protect himself but he still hit the steps hard. He felt the world spin, and each step on his back and shoulders, as he tumbled to the bottom. He would have lain there and breathed his last if Zac didn't heave him to his feet one more time.

"You're almost there—come on!"

Through a haze of suffering, Matthew saw the back door on the other side of the kitchen.

"Last chance!" Zac whispered.

Matthew hobbled forward, one step and then another. Zac's breath was a constant companion in his ear. He reached out like a blind man, to steady himself on the dining table. The back door was a beacon. Moments passed like hours as he carried his battered body toward it. He felt sorry for himself, but mostly he felt sorry for leaving his mother behind.

"You'll let me go?"

"Sure. Go on." Zac snapped his fingers and pointed at the door.

Matthew took one final rickety step and turned the handle. The door opened wide. Darkness seeped into the Campbell home like a wave of oil. The room, and everything within, decayed before Matthew's eyes in moments. He staggered through the doorway, trying to understand how one house could be inside another.

Cold steel slipped inside Matthew's lower back. Zac's arm wrapped around his chest in a queer embrace as the knife was driven all the way to the hilt. A geyser of blood filled Matthew's mouth and he began to choke.

"This is *my* house," Zac said. "Do you like it?"

Matthew slumped into his brother's arms as the coldness of the blade spread. His breaths became shallow as he beheld the house next door.

"No one ever leaves Eric Kemper's house. None of you will," Zac continued. "Soon, every house in this street will be shining temples to the dark. And upon innocent blood, I will build his church."

When he pulled the knife free, Matthew fell, and his blood— his soul—bled in between the floorboards of the Kemper House.

CHAPTER EIGHTEEN

Richard Markham awoke to find himself alive.

The room was pitch-black and the sheets around him were damp with sweat. He stretched out an arm to touch his wife, but Margaret's side of the bed was even colder. Mentally, he felt much better, the feverish dreams and visions were gone, but now his Margaret was nowhere to be seen.

He shuffled across the floor and felt for the nearest wall, trying to discern why it was so dark.

Perhaps it was just an old fool's eyes, the same eyes that had earlier believed he'd been back in Iwo Jima fighting Japs, when instead he was at home, on good old Willow Street. Still, he could find no comfort without his wife.

"Margie?" he called out. "Margie, are you in the kitchen?" His fingertips found nothing but the air around him. The wall should have been a few steps away. "Where's the damn light switch?"

Richard's eyes adjusted, providing him shapes and the dull edges of objects. His house had never looked so foreign, so dark. He felt like he was in the dream again, inside that foul house where he'd seen the boy—

The boy, one of the Campbell boys, yes, that was him. What on earth was *he* doing in his dream about that blasted house?

Richard stopped and took a slow breath as an epiphany struck him. Was he dreaming again? Or was he back in his bed, still experiencing a fever dream? He needed to feel something to know. His eyesight was not enough. He needed all of his senses to discover where he was.

His hearing had taken a bit of a beating during the war, but in the empty darkness, the sounds came to him. He heard his heartbeat and breathing. He heard the creak of floorboards under his feet. Beyond that, there was nothing.

Richard took a deep breath. The taint of dust and mildew filled his nostrils. But there was something else that revealed itself in the murk. In the jungles he'd learned to smell for the enemy, to smell for cigarettes, or shit, and piss, and he smelled one of those distinct aromas at that very moment. He turned to his right and followed his nose. If he was dreaming, perhaps he would come to understand their messages and find a way back to Margaret.

He followed the darkened trail, letting his feet map out the path. His sense of foreboding was the same fear-inducing, soul-weakening sensation he'd experienced on the battlefield. The only difference was on the battlefield he knew his enemy.

The scent of blood slowly overpowered all other aromas, and his fear reached its threshold. He scanned the black with his old eyes, suddenly fearing the worst for his wife.

"Margie?" he muttered.

He heard the sound of someone gasping, and on instinct, the former soldier dropped on arthritic knees in readiness for an impending attack. He swiped his palms along the floor desperate to feel some connection to the real world.

"Margie, I'm here. It's Richard." The coppery stink clung to his nostrils. He knew he was close. "Are you hurt?" His fingertips smeared against a cold and viscous substance. He gasped for breath. "Oh, God!"

He begged for some source of light as he reached out to grip the body lying before him.

"Margie... no!"

The old man frowned. The body felt far too muscular to be his wife, and the shocking realization made him withdraw his hands.

"Oh, God! Are... are you alright?"

The body gasped again, the gasps of the dying. The sticky pool of blood was wide, and Richard knew that whoever this person was, they were at death's door.

"I'll get help," Richard said, forgetting he was still inside a dream.

The darkness withdrew with a snap, as a fireplace erupted

with flame. The old man looked down, horrified at the sight of a teenage boy, a knife protruding from his back.

"Mother of God!"

"She's not here," a voice answered.

Richard saw another boy standing in the light of the fireplace. His hands were caked in blood; his smile was like an open wound.

"You're back," the boy said. "And I see you've found young Matthew."

The old man looked from the boy's hands to the dead boy's wounds. "You killed him?"

"Technically, no…"

Richard recognised the Campbell boy—the one who'd appeared in his previous dream. Zachary Campbell. He lifted himself to his feet and stepped away from the younger boy's corpse. He strained to remember the other Campbell boy's name. "Matthew," he said finally.

"My baby brother." Zac put on a sad face.

Richard remembered the Campbell brothers riding their bicycles up and down the street during summer, their young voices carrying in the humid air. He recalled how seeing them made him long to be a father. "This is a dream." Richard said, raising his eyes to Zac's. "Why would I dream about you killing your brother?"

Zac cocked his head. "Are you sure it's a dream?"

Richard looked around the room. "This isn't my house, and I saw you before in my last dream."

"Maybe you're still having it. Or maybe you're dead and this is the dream you have when you die."

Again that lascivious smile; Richard straightened and puffed out his chest. "I know this isn't real. It's the Kemper House. I'm sick, and I've had that house on my mind."

Zac raised a bloody finger. "The house made you sick? It certainly made Zac sick, and Matthew, and Amy."

Richard frowned at the boy's words; he didn't speak like a teenager, nor did he act like one. "If you've got something meaningful to say, then hurry up and say it, because I'd like to go back to sleep."

"If you say so, Richy-Rich-Rich." Zac walked towards him, and yanked the knife from Matthew's back. The blood on the tip of the blade was almost black. Richard took several steps back, which appeared to make Zac curious. "Why are you afraid if this is just a dream?"

"Isn't that the point of nightmares—to scare?" He looked at the house with its peeling, shadowed walls. "Haunted houses are all the same."

"This house isn't haunted," Zac said. "It's empty, but soon it's going to be full, and when it is, I'll be made anew."

Richard looked into the boy's eyes. They were grey, and refused to refract any light, like they belonged to something that should have been dead. "Who are you?"

Zac smiled. "Don't you want to know where Margaret is?"

Richard's heart quickened. "She's not here... because this is a dream."

Zac shook his head. "She's down the hall, back in your room."

"This isn't my house!"

"This *is* your house, but it no longer belongs to you. None of these houses do. They belong to the one I worship. The one I serve."

"I've had enough! You don't know where my wife is because this is a dream!" Richard started to walk away, but Zac blocked his path, the knife held firmly in his hand.

"Your wife is down the hall, sound asleep," the boy said. "I'll show you."

Richard pushed Zac aside. He wasn't afraid of a figment of his imagination any longer. "Get out of my way! Get out of my head."

"You think you can just walk back to your room and wake up? Things don't work like that anymore. Come on, let's go wake up Margie and see what she has to say about you being out of bed."

The boy smiled and then broke into a run, his knife-wielding arm whipping through the air. The hallway seemed to swallow him up, but his laughter carried long and loud back to Richard, who shivered with doubt. The old man gave chase on aching knees, until he tripped on his slippers and slammed against the wall and its ancient paint, which crackled into a thousand pieces. The paint crumbled to dust on his fingertips, and he tried to fathom how it felt so real. Had he truly smelled the other Campbell boy's blood? Was this still his house?

Richard ran as fast as he could down the hall. When he reached the doorway he was shocked to see his bedroom on the other side—and Zac leering over his sleeping wife. The boy held his bloodied knife against one of her closed eyelids.

"Don't you hurt her!" Richard said, stepping into the room. His wife never even flinched at his outburst.

Zac pressed a finger to his lips. "She's sleeping."

Richard moved closer, torn between rushing in and not escalating the situation. Yet his mind kept trying to convince him it was only a dream. "Move away from her!" He looked at Margaret, silently praying for her to stay asleep.

"She thinks you're going crazy, do you know that, Richy?" Zac said, looking down on the old woman.

"You shut your mouth. You don't know anything about her!"

"Oh, but I know everything about Margie. She's frightened you're going to hurt her. She doesn't understand why you won't go to the doctor."

"Get out of my house!"

"I told you—you're in His house now!"

Zac raised the knife above Margaret's rising chest and Richard leapt in. The old man summoned some hidden strength and pulled the knife free from the teenager's hands. He dragged Zac onto the bed and held him down.

"I'm going to kill you, you little shit!"

Richard drove the knife into Zac's chest again and again, until a torrent of blood escaped from the boy's lips. The veteran could almost feel the stock of his rifle, the length of the bayonet driving home to twist the enemy's innards until they ruptured. His chest heaved with satisfaction as the boy breathed his last.

"Ri... Richard?"

He looked down at the face of his victim and screamed. Margaret gazed up at him, mouthing wordlessly as her blood spread onto the bedding. Her eyes were wide with disbelief and betrayal.

"Margie!" Richard cried. "Margie!"

He recoiled from what he'd done and searched the room for proof he was still dreaming. But all he saw was Zachary Campbell, standing at the foot of the bed, smiling.

The old man's heart stopped.

Darryl Novak snapped the lock shut and felt the cold caress of the bunker against his skin and it helped ease the fear that had gripped his heart.

He'd never run so fast in all his life, but he was so relieved to be back home, safe and sound. He didn't know why he'd gone to stare at that woman, Megan at number 70. It was if he'd awoken and just found himself there. Darryl never did that. He never looked through windows. When he "worked," it was always on the street at night, from the safety of his car. She wasn't even his type, so what the hell had he been doing there?

The shape he'd seen in the backyard—and the voice—had put him off his game and it showed. His hands trembled and his upper lip was heavy with sweat. He didn't like to feel afraid. Not being in control was his one true weakness, one that he thought he'd conquered. Since his mother's death *he* had been the one in control, taking what he wanted, when he wanted it, and never worrying about the consequences. The thing in the backyard—whatever it was—had reminded him otherwise.

There was no denying what he'd seen and heard, but he'd put it down to stress. It wasn't that the kind of stress his dear mother had put him under, but rather the stress of not being able to indulge. In the half-light of the bunker, Darryl squeezed his hand into a fist, so tight the skin flared white. When he released his fingers the trembling was gone, and this made him smile. He could get back to doing what he did best, and the vision he'd experienced in the yard would trouble him no more.

He walked down the narrow concrete hall and switched on the overhead lights. They flickered on and off like a strobe and then reached full intensity, casting his raggedy doll's naked form in a sickly light. He gave her a quick glance; smiling at how she slumped in the chains, admiring the way the crude make-up belied her defeated expression. He approached a table where his tools and iPod dock sat. He swiped through the iPod to his favourite playlist and pressed play. Trumpets began to blare, and the girl awoke with a scream.

Darryl swayed and danced as Dean Martin sang. He was light on his feet despite his heavy build. "Everybody loves somebody, sometime," he crooned, almost as well as Mr. Martin. The woman recoiled and let out a series of shrill cries, but Darryl just kept on singing. "Everyone falls in love somehow..."

The girl's painted eyes widened in their sockets. She screamed and sobbed at his display. Darryl gripped her chains and swayed her from side to side to the music. He savoured every sliver of her terror. "Something in your kiss just told me... that sometime is now..."

He tried to press his lips to hers. She wrenched her head away. "No!"

A wave of heat flushed across Darryl's chest. He looked at her and imagined her real mouth all bloody and broken, and saw himself stitching it back together again. Scowling, he strode to the table and paused Dean, just as the singer entered the second chorus.

"You're ruining the song," he said through gritted teeth. The girl whimpered and he felt his cock harden. He knew she knew what was coming. "I'm only trying to set a mood here," he said. "Why do you have to make such a fuss?" He ran his eyes over her simpering form, admiring the purple and yellow blotches on her ribs, the bite marks he'd administered on her breasts days before. "Are you going to be quiet and listen to Dean? Hmm?"

The girl's whimpering faded.

"That's better." He reached for the iPod and pressed play. Mr. Martin continued to tell the world about how everybody loved somebody sometime.

A pounding on the bunker door froze him to the spot.

The girl looked up. "Help!" she cried, but before she could utter another word, Darryl cracked her across the jaw with the back of his hand. She went limp in her chains.

He looked to the steps leading to the bunker door. His heart pounded in his ears. Who would dare knock on the door? Who would dare trespass on his property? He snatched a rusty wrench from the table and tip-toed to the door, when a shard of fear twisted in his head.

What if it's that thing, again?

BANG-BANG-BANG!

Darryl swallowed his fear and tightened his grip on the wrench. He knew he was stronger than this, and his mother had always told him not to be a coward. He decided to stay quiet, with the hope that whoever it was outside would go away.

BANG-BANG-BANG!

Every beat sent a jolt through him.

Don't be so weak! His mother screamed in the back of his mind.

He yelled and ran up the stairs. With the wrench raised in one hand, he opened the door with the other. Moonlight poured in, but it failed to illuminate the trespasser. Darryl took a deep breath and stepped into the backyard, his wrench still at the ready.

"Who's there? I'll call the police!"

"If you do that, they'll find out about your lady friend." It was the voice, the same one he'd heard earlier in the evening; a boy's voice.

"Get off my property!" Darryl yelled back.

The voice let out a derisive snort. "Your mommy's house, you mean."

"Don't you talk about my mother!"

Laughter filled the air and whisked by him like a passing bullet. Darryl whirled, and realised he'd left the bunker door wide open. He looked inside and saw a shape bundling down the stairs.

"No!" He gave chase and almost tripped. The wrench felt loose in his sweaty palm. "You're not allowed down here!" Down the hall, his rag doll screamed anew, but it wasn't Darryl who was imbuing her with a fresh wave of fear. When he rounded the corner, he saw the boy, standing behind his prized possession. He had a tooth-filled grin on his face.

"You've been naughty, haven't you Darryl?" the boy said.

Darryl held the wrench out, wishing he'd grabbed his knife instead. The boy was unmoved, and was highly amused, going by the look on his face. The teenager's hands were covered in dried blood and more of it was spattered across his shirt.

"Get out of here—whoever you are!"

The boy produced a bloodied knife from behind his back. He poked the tip of it into the girl's neck. She squealed, her eyes so wide they could have popped from her skull. "I'm here to help you Darryl—to give you a little push," the boy said.

"Shut up!" He stepped forward but stopped when the boy's knife drew blood from the woman's filthy skin. Darryl felt his face flush and his blood quicken. "Stop that! She's mine!"

"Oh, this one's just a play-thing. You and I both know that," the boy said. "She's just like all the others you've brought down here. But I'm here to tell you that the real prize is just down the road."

Darryl could hardly think. "Stop it! Just stop talking!"

"Darryl," the boy sighed and walked around the other side of the girl. Terrified, she couldn't take her eyes off him, as if Darryl was no longer in the room. "I know all about you," he said. "You see, I've been watching you ever since you were a boy living with your mother in this little cottage, and I've seen you grow, fed on a daily diet of verbal and physical abuse. It made you the man you are today."

Darryl shook his head. How could this child know a thing about him? "You shut your mouth you little shit, or I'll bash your fucking head in!" He raised the wrench, but the boy simply tut-tutted him with a wagging finger.

"That's not your style, is it? Besides, you won't kill me, because you're intrigued by what I have to offer."

"You're just a kid. What could you possibly have to offer me?"

"Years of experience—literally hundreds of years," the boy said. "This is just the small stuff. It barely scratches the surface of the kind of power you could wield." The boy held up his blood-caked hand and clenched it into a fist. "You dream of holding one soul in your hand—imagine if you could hold all of them. All that blood. All that flesh." He gripped the girl's hair and she whimpered. "This is just a taste of what you could have."

Darryl ogled the boy's sweaty face, and his wild eyes. But he didn't see conviction; all he saw was insanity. The kid was obviously high on something. Darryl spat on the floor. "Enough talk. I don't fucking care who or what you think you are. You come into my home—you die!" He moved in, but the boy only shook his head in disappointment.

"It looks like it's time to teach you a lesson."

The knife slid into the girl's throat and a spurt of blood followed, redder than any lipstick he could ever hope to smear. It sprayed across Darryl's shirt and trousers, hot and wet. He let out a high-pitched cry as his raggedy doll choked on the flow of it. All he could do now was watch, as the girl's bruises were covered in red, and his pleasure was stolen by the rapidly-fading pumps of her terrified heart. "You took her from me! She was mine! Fucking mine!"

The spreading pool of blood ignited the monster in Darryl and he launched himself at the boy. The pair crashed onto the concrete in a flail of limbs, and it took him no time at all to find the boy's throat between his fingers. "I'm going to fucking kill you!"

The boy smiled and wheezed. "That's... the spirit."

Darryl's knuckles burned as he squeezed the boy's throat, but his exertions, his rage, had no effect. He tightened his grip until he could feel the contours of the boy's vertebrae. Still, the boy laughed.

"Come on Darryl. You have to want this."

"Just fucking die!" Darryl's spittle fell on the boy's cheek and trailed down into his grinning mouth. He couldn't understand why his voice remained unaffected.

"You first!" The boy stared up at him, his face carved with macabre glee.

Darryl's fingers flexed open and he knew he was longer in control of his own body. Every muscle in his body became rigid. His back arched inward like he'd been struck by lightning. A stream of piss ran down the inside of his trouser leg. Paralysed, he could only watch as the boy reached up with his blood-caked hands, plunged his fingers deep into Darryl's mouth, and pried his jaw apart. The boy's mouth spread open. Black smoke wisped out like a cobra; it smelled of charred flesh. Darryl would have gagged if his guts weren't as hard as rock.

He felt the smoke crawl down his throat, invading his insides. And when it found his soul, the last thing Darryl saw, in his feeble, narcissistic mind, was his mother swimming in a sea of darkness, her finger crooked to summon him like she used to when he was about to be punished. And this time, the punishment would be eternal.

Megan had her bags packed; all she had to do was walk out the door. So why couldn't she? Why couldn't she take the next step?

She grabbed her phone off the kitchen counter. She dialled for a taxi and realised it was the second time she'd made the attempt. Maybe it was the memory of her neighbour, screaming for help. Losing a child—Megan could barely imagine the pain, whereas not having one at all was something she knew all too well.

She would have had Ben's children if he'd wanted them. At least that's how she'd felt when they first met, before he put his career before her. In many ways she was glad she hadn't put herself through motherhood because in the end it would have been the kid who'd suffered. This way, their parting would only affect them, and not some innocent child.

The sound of breaking glass turned Megan away from the phone and her morbid thoughts. Through the window, she glimpsed her neighbour, Alice Cowley, struggling to carry several cardboard boxes to her car. One of the boxes had fallen, spilling delicate contents over the driveway. Megan slipped her phone into her jacket and hurried to the front door. She jogged up the path to help the woman, who was crying all over again. China cups and saucers were spread out in pieces at the woman's feet.

"Here, let me help you." Megan bent to pick up the fragments.

The woman stared blankly. "Oh... thank you," she said.

Megan admired the floral pattern on the china plates and

felt a pang of regret as she caught a glimpse of the woman's tears. "I'm so sorry. And I'm sorry about your daughter."

The woman cradled the broken pieces of plate. She nodded her thanks.

"My name's Megan. Megan Traynor."

"Alice. Alice Cowley."

"Mom?"

Megan looked up to see a boy holding a box of his own. His eyes also registered loss.

"This is my son Dale," Alice said. "Dale, could you go and grab a dustpan, please?"

Dale put his box down and walked back inside the house.

"You're moving away?"

"I... we just can't live here anymore."

"I'm moving out, too."

Alice frowned. "You are?"

"I'm splitting up with my husband."

"Oh, I'm so sorry."

Dale came back, dustpan in hand. His mother took it and started to sweep up the smaller pieces. "I can clean up the rest," Alice said. "Thanks for your help Megan—and your compassion."

Megan squeezed Alice's hand. "I just wanted to help, and to say how sorry I am."

Alice nodded. "Thank you. And good luck to you."

Megan walked back towards her house, the guilt of not knowing Alice and her family before, weighing hard on her shoulders. It was easier for people not to care about others; to limit the circle of pain. Her expression of sympathy had been too little and too late, but she hoped that Alice knew she'd been sincere. She glanced over Willow Street and thought about all the other people she was about to leave behind. Megan wished them luck, too.

She stopped suddenly, thinking she'd seen someone standing behind a tree across the street, someone watching her. A second look convinced Megan it was just her imagination, and she went inside her house, shaking her head at her gullibility.

CHAPTER NINETEEN

Ben's skull blazed with agony when he regained consciousness. He looked around the darkened room with blurry eyes. Pulsing pain shot through his temple, and when he clamped his hand on it to quell its intensity, his palm came away with blood. The sight of glistening red on his skin brought his last memory to the surface.

"Mitchell, Mitchell Cross." The last thing he'd seen was the madman stepping out of the dark. He tried to get to his feet but the throbbing inside his head, left him weak. Cross had hit him hard.

"I told you not to go into that house."

Ben flinched as Cross emerged from behind a row of standing shelves filled with archive boxes, the length of pipe still in his hand. "You keep back!"

"Why did you go in there? I warned you not to go in there."

Cross's hospital gown was a different shade to Ben's, off-white, with flecks of dirt and other stains. The man paced on the spot and picked at his skin with dirty fingernails. He had descended even farther into madness since Ben had first met him at *The Gazette*. Cross had gone to the extreme by taking Ben captive, but Ben didn't know whether he was in a storage room or hospital basement. The room they were in was just shelves of archive boxes, leading off to a door. Through a small window in the door, Ben could make out a flight of stairs.

"Look, you need to calm down, Mitchell," Ben said. "Just take it easy."

Cross ran a shaky hand through his hair and pulled at the strands. "The house isn't safe! Not my house, and not the one on Willow Street!" He looked up. "Not even this building is safe!"

"Okay, then let's get out of here. Let's go somewhere where we can talk."

"No!" Cross trembled with rage. "You can't leave! If you leave, the house will claim you."

Ben got on his haunches. He had to be ready to make a run for it if Cross became violent, and the look in his eyes told him he wasn't far off. "I have to leave. I have to warn others about the Willow Street house. Just like you warned me."

"I warned you, but you still went in there. Why would you be so stupid!?"

"I wanted to know the truth about what happened to your family. Now I know."

Cross grimaced, baring yellow teeth. "You didn't believe me?"

"No, no I did believe you. I just wanted to see what the house was like—inside."

"That's because it wanted you to! You shouldn't have gone there!"

"The house is gone now. It burned down."

A hint of elation passed over Cross' features, but it quickly faded to sorrow. "You burned it?"

"There was an electrical fault. When I flicked one of the switches, it sparked and started a fire."

Cross licked his lips, his eyes narrowing. "You're lying. Why are you lying?" He took two steps closer and Ben stood straight.

"No, I'm telling the truth…"

"You saw something in that house, didn't you?"

Ben pressed his back against the wall. "It was empty."

Cross shook his head. "They're never empty. What did you see?" The madman took another step closer.

"Nothing, I swear."

Cross grabbed Ben by the shirt and shook him. There was no rage in Cross' eyes, only desperation. He raised the pipe in his other hand. "It showed you what it wanted you to see! You shouldn't have looked! You shouldn't have gone in there."

"I know, I know and I'm sorry," Ben said. "Please you have to let me go so I can warn everyone. My wife is across the street from that house. I have to make sure she's okay. Please!"

Mitchell shook him again. "Your wife's already dead! Everyone on that street is dead!"

Ben shoved Cross backward. The man slammed into one of the shelves, spilling two boxes of hospital files onto the floor. Ben heard Cross' weapon hit the ground with a clang, echoing away as it rolled along the concrete floor. "Megan's not going to end up like your wife, trapped in that hell-hole! I'm going to go to that house and burn it down, too!"

Cross' eyes widened. "So you *did* burn it down!"

Ben silently cursed his own foolishness. "I told you it was an accident!"

"What did you see?" Cross attacked Ben again, but this time his hands were wrapped around his throat. "Did you see Cindy? Nathan? Did you see my little boy?"

"No..."

"Did you burn that house down with my family inside!?"

Ben gasped for breath. "They... they were already... dead."

"No! Nooo!" Cross lashed out with a fist to Ben's face.

The reporter's vision wavered from the force of the blow, but Ben's desire to fight and flee was enough to keep him standing. He smashed his left elbow into Cross' nose. The man stumbled backward, a torrent of blood splashing over his gown. Ben took the opportunity to kick his shocked opponent in the knee, and Cross buckled to the floor. But when Ben tried to plant another kick to his ribs, the man was waiting and grabbed the reporter's leg dropping him on his back. Cross crawled across the floor, quick as a snake, once more wrapping his thin hands around Ben's neck.

"I can't let you leave! The house knows you. It sees you!"

Ben saw blasts of blackness behind his eyes as Cross squeezed his throat. The reporter's lungs burned for air, and through a fog of asphyxiation, Ben summoned the last of his strength to scratch at Cross' grimacing face. Ben's fingertips became slick with blood. Cross howled and loosened his grip, and the reporter was able to bring his knee into the madman's groin. He shoved Cross aside and ran to open the door and make for the stairs.

Cross' moans of agony became shrieks of rage which

followed Ben's every step. He knew Cross would pursue him, but all he had to do was get to the next floor and signal for help. His half-crushed throat seared with each frantic breath, but he had to keep going. He had to get out of the hospital and back home, and send that house back to Hell where it belonged.

A scream and slap of feet on the stairs below pushed Ben on more urgently. He turned left onto one flight of stairs, and then right onto another, until he finally reached the door to the next floor. To his horror, the door was locked. He pulled on the handle and screamed for help, but those on the other side seemed deaf to his pleas.

"You can't leave!"

Ben turned just as Cross tackled him. They fell to the floor. Cross had the upper hand, and powered by his psychosis, rained down a series of punches into his face. Ben felt his nose break, and he tasted blood at the back of his throat. He lifted his knees and kicked out, sending Cross toppling back down the stairs. The man tumbled against the concrete, until his agonised cries were silenced by the sickening snap of bone.

Bruised and bloodied, Ben crawled to the edge of the steps and saw his attacker lying at the bottom, his neck broken. Cross' eyes stared blankly into Ben's own. Ben turned away and breathed. He was alive, and there was still a chance to save himself, and his wife, from the curse of Willow Street. Groaning, he pulled himself to his feet and got ready to bang on the door again for help—when suddenly, it opened.

To Ben's bemusement there was no one on the other side, and as he made a run for the hospital's front doors, not a single, solitary soul was there to stop him.

Bags in hand, Megan opened the front door, only to find a strange, short, chubby man standing at the other side.

The man adjusted the glasses on his nose and smiled. "Hello."

"Oh, you startled me." Megan looked the man up and down. "Can I help you?"

The man smiled again. "My name's Darryl, and I live down the street at Number 61."

Megan placed her bags on the floor and offered Darryl the plainest smile she could muster.

"Hi," she said.

The man raised his eyebrows and nodded. "I just thought I'd come and introduce myself, you know, be a good neighbour."

"Well, thank you, but as you can see," she indicated the bags. "I'm about to leave."

Darryl didn't even glance at the bags; he just kept on smiling, and Megan felt a twinge of apprehension. "Are you going on vacation?" Darryl said.

"Um… sort of. Look, I'm sorry, but I'm waiting for my taxi."

"Oh, how rude of me," Darryl chuckled. "I was just, you know, trying to be a better neighbour." He put on a more serious face. "Especially with all the terrible things that have been happening." He looked briefly over his shoulder at the dark house across the street. "It's just awful, and with poor Amy Cowley taking her life… so tragic."

Megan glanced at the Kemper House and back to Darryl. The sad look he was giving her, made his face look even chubbier, and she wasn't entirely sure he was being sincere. "Yes, it has been very hard." She picked up her bags. "I appreciate you coming over, but I really have to go."

Darryl made a grab for her suitcase. "Let me help."

"No it's fine, really. I can manage." She picked up her bags and stepped out of the doorway.

Darryl grabbed her wrist. "You won't even tell me your name, you ungrateful bitch?" His eyes grew cold. Megan attempted to scream, but her neighbour clamped a sweaty hand over her mouth. "But it doesn't matter anyway because I know everything about you, don't I, Megan?"

He shoved her so hard she struck her head on the tiled floor and plunged into a black pool of unconsciousness.

Ben drove his car to the limit, weaving between cars on the freeway. He didn't care if the police tried to stop him. He hoped a patrol car would spot him and give chase, just so he could lead them home.

When Megan told him she was leaving, Ben had felt crushed.

But now, with all that was happening around the Kemper House, he wanted her to be gone, to be out of harm's way.

If the house got a hold of his wife…

But he couldn't think like that. He had to focus, and figure out a way to stop the evil from spreading.

As he drove, he wondered if he was already too late. The Kemper House and its evil had existed long before anyone in the city was even born; its roots were firmly planted and stretched in every direction. He knew from his experience at the Mayne Avenue address that the Kemper House held sway over death; that those who died inside were doomed to reside within for all eternity and do the bidding of some demonic entity.

The blare of a car horn wrenched his thoughts back to the road. Ben swerved in front of a sedan and sped up the outside lane to overtake a cement truck. He was touching 90 miles per hour. He'd never driven this fast in his entire life. But then, he'd never held so many lives in his hands. He shook his head, still disbelieving.

Was this what it was like in Mitchell Cross' head? And his wife's, before she killed her only son?

Cross' final words came to him again and the fear along with it.

What if this was the house's doing? What if it wanted him to race home? What if this was all part of its plan?

No, he told himself. *You're in control. Just get to the house and burn it to the ground. Send it back to Hell.*

Seeing the exit ahead, Ben steered the car into the inside lane and then floored it to overtake another vehicle. He exited the freeway and started to count down the miles to Willow Street.

Megan opened her eyes and found the world around her so dark and cold she thought she was already dead. When she tried to sit up her head pounded, and she had to take a deep breath to stifle the nausea that hit her like a wave. She squeezed her eyes shut and re-opened them, hoping that miraculously everything would return to normal, but she was betrayed by the stark reality of her surroundings. She was no longer in her own house.

Wet warmth trickled down the back of her neck. She tried to move her hand to touch it and was shocked to find her hands were fastened behind her back. The skin of her wrists stung when she tried to wriggle them free. The nausea settled deeper in her gut, roiling into a pulse of fear. Her heart pounded faster and her head throbbed in turn as she realised the danger she was in.

Through the murk of dizziness, Megan tried to recognise the room. The air was musty, the floor beneath her gritty and worn, the walls were cracked and peeling. The entire space contained only the faintest hint of light, a shaft of moonlight creeping between the heavy curtains that covered every window. She didn't know which house she was in, but she could guess how she'd arrived inside its foreign walls. The ache on the back of her head brought with it a memory of the man who had attacked her.

Darryl.

He appeared from around a corner as if summoned by her thoughts. Megan recoiled and felt the skin of her wrists tear as she tried to move away from him. Even in the dark she could make out his round face and equally circular glasses. She remembered his face now; he was the man she met in the street the day the body was found, and the man at her window. The lenses reflected Megan's horrified gaze.

"You're awake," he said. "Excellent."

"Stay away from me!" Megan squirmed.

Darryl stood at her feet and slipped his hands into his pockets.

She dreaded what he might have concealed in them.

"I'm not going anywhere." He smiled and readjusted his glasses. "I've waited a very long time for this moment."

Megan screamed, as loud and long as she could. "Help me! Help!" Her voice swirled around the room but faded as soon as she ran out of breath.

Darryl laughed. "Are you done?"

"Fuck you!"

"You can scream all you like. He laughed again. No one will hear you. This house is completely empty."

"They'll hear me outside! Help me! Help!"

Her kidnapper shook his head. "This is His house. It stands outside this world. It only reveals itself to those it deems worthy. It is his temple."

Megan thought he sounded like Ben. The only difference was that Darryl had already lost his mind. "What do you want with me?"

Darryl smirked and sat in a cracked leather recliner. A great waft of dust painted the moonlit air around him. "To serve the purpose all women serve," Darryl said.

Megan swallowed. She knew what he intended and fought to contain her fear. "I won't let you touch me."

"When you understand your purpose, I believe you'll go willingly."

Megan clenched her jaw. "Just fucking try it." Her thoughts trailed back to Ben, and how she wished he were here. She felt tears in her eyes and dared herself not to blink, not to let them fall.

Darryl expanded his hands and gazed about the room. "I built this house so long ago." he said. "I came here—to America—to start anew. I'd hoped to bring his vision with me, to be his apostle. People back then had nothing but their faith. Christians, Jews, Protestants, Masons. I wanted to spread the true word, and show people that they should embrace darkness rather than fear it. A few came into the church, but it was all too secretive, going out at night, meeting in cramped drawing rooms and halls. I used my gift as an architect to find employment with the local council, and it wasn't long before I had the ear of the Mayor. Just a few words was all it took in those days. People were hungry for guidance, for signs and wonders and oh—they saw many." He was suddenly downcast. "But, by venturing into the squalor of this city I succumbed to its filth. Months after coming here I fell ill. At first I was enraged; I felt betrayed by Him. But as I slowly weakened, I realised that He'd bestowed on me a gift—a purpose. So I channelled my pain into building temples. I shared my plans with the Mayor, and the doctors and benefactors I had secured, and they helped me build His Houses."

Megan looked to the ceiling, and the fireplace and saw how old they were. "This is the house across the street?"

"Indeed," Darryl said. "But it's more than just a house. Behind these walls is a welcoming darkness." He nodded toward the moonlight splitting the curtain. "Through those windows you will see him." He gestured to the staircase. "And up those stairs, he is waiting to take you into his arms—if you'll let him."

Megan had no desire to understand Darryl's insanity, but she had to if she wanted to survive. She prayed Ben hadn't heeded her goodbyes. "So, he's some sort of god?"

Darryl leaned forward. The leather chair creaked. "There *are* no gods," he said. "Only darkness and light."

"And you're a worshipper?"

"I am his vessel here on earth. By building his temples, he granted me resurrection so I could continue to spread his word and grant him more souls."

"But you can't have built this place. It's too old."

Darryl stood and smoothed back his balding pate. "He resurrected my soul, not my body. Darryl is purely a shell, but in time this body too will wither and die." He crouched to grab her bonds and pull her to her feet. Megan gasped. "Which is where you come in, my dear."

CHAPTER TWENTY

The hills were silhouettes against the dawn, but even Ben could see the Kemper House was the greater monument to time.

Ben stepped out of the Jeep, mesmerised by the structure that had taken over his mind, his life. He studied the street. Each house seemed an extension of the older house, like megalithic stones on an endless plain. The birds didn't sing and there was no wind, not a sound, and it was at this moment that Ben feared he was too late; that every soul had been lost to Kemper's evil. He looked upon the house with hatred.

"I'm going to burn you to the fucking ground," he said.

A sudden chill breeze buffeted Ben's face and he couldn't help but feel it was the house laughing at him.

Shivering, he closed the car door and turned his back on the building. He walked across the street to *his* house, thinking about his plans. His own home was quiet, the curtains drawn, the door closed.

The Kemper House always looked that way too. Lurking in silence.

He put his key in the lock, and looked over his shoulder at the black edifice across the street. He twisted the key, a slight smile on his face. The Kemper House didn't know what was coming.

Ben opened the door, stepped into the foyer and dropped his keys to the floor. The front door slammed closed behind him. His house had been hollowed out; replaced with the crumbling insides of another, one built from darkness. Panic set in as he understood where he was. He whirled back to the door, pulling on the handle to no avail. His house had become the Kemper House and it wasn't about to let him leave.

"Fuck!" He slammed his palm against the door. Flecks of paint crumbled to the dust-covered floor. He looked around the foyer, trying to decide what to do. The space surrounding him was dark, and when he parted one of the curtains to look outside, he discovered the Kemper House was even defying the rising sun. He saw only stars in an ebony sky. Everything about the house was impossible, but Ben hadn't believed in ghosts either until four of them had tried to kill him. Cursing his misfortune and stupidity, he scooped the keys off the floor and put them in his jacket pocket.

"Ok, you've got me. Now what?"

The fireplace in the living room erupted with a whoosh of flame. Ben stared at the fire and saw it did little to light the room.

"Neat trick," he said. "But that's all this is—trickery."

Floorboards creaked.

Ben stiffened in readiness, his heart flooding with adrenalin. *Fight or flee.*

He knew full well the house was locked tighter than a tomb.

A figure appeared from around a corner, a short man dressed in a woollen three-piece suit.

"This way," the man said, and about-faced before Ben could object.

The reporter didn't move at first, and listened as the footsteps moved away. The sound of the footfalls swelled and mingled with other sounds—voices—men talking. Ben took a step in their direction, his desire for answers overcoming his instinct's need to escape. He could feel the house reaching out to him, and swallowing his trepidation, he followed in the man's wake and entered the drawing room.

A group of men, thirteen of them, huddled together around a table, dressed in suits and frock coats. Wafts of tobacco smoke hovered in the air like a storm cloud. They whispered to each other and sipped from crystal glasses. But only the man Ben had first encountered bothered to acknowledge him.

"You're just in time, Mr. Traynor," the man said.

The rest of the group turned to look at him.

Ben approached, intent on getting a glimpse of what lay

within their circle. "What's going on? How did I get here?"

"All in good time," the first man said.

He regarded the men carefully, the cut of their jackets, the fob watches in their vests. One man wore a monocle. "Who are you people?"

"This is my home," the man said.

"But it is His temple," said the others in unison.

It became hard to breathe. The men were close. They stood tall and patient. Still, Ben wanted to know what they were hiding. He stepped forward and tried to push them aside, but they jostled together like links in a chain. He felt a hand grip his shoulder, and found the man with the accent at his back.

"She is no longer your wife, Mr. Traynor," he said. "She belongs to Him."

An ache settled inside Ben's head. "What?"

"She was born for this moment," one of the other men said.

"A divine purpose," said another.

Ben's chest tightened. He needed to know what was behind the wall of madmen. "What are you hiding?"

He leapt at them and met a wall of resistance. The men were stronger than they appeared. Although he couldn't get through, he saw more than enough.

"Megan!"

"Ben!"

Megan saw the terror in her husband's eyes as he struggled. The men held him firmly, and pulled him away from the circle.

"What are you doing to my wife!?" Ben said, thrashing against them.

Megan's naked body shivered beneath the creeping cold, beneath bonds that lashed her to the table. All she could move was her lips.

"Ben, stop!" she said, trying to calm him.

Instead, he struck one of the men in the jaw. He lurched forward, but two more of the group were quick to restrain him. Their leader slapped him hard across the face and her husband fell to his knees.

"You should listen to your wife, Mr. Traynor," the man said.

"There is nothing you can do to prevent this. The moment has long been prepared for."

"I'm going to kill you!" Ben yelled.

Megan was terrified by the hatred in his eyes.

"I'm going to kill all of you!"

"Shall we begin, Mr. Kemper?" another of the group said.

Megan's heart quickened. She saw the same look of disbelief cross her husband's stricken face.

"You're Kemper?" Ben tried to regain his feet, but the men shoved him back down.

Kemper removed his coat and handed it to one of his party. "This is my house," he repeated. "I built it for Him, and in return he gave me eternal life." He slipped off his suspenders and began to unbutton his shirt. "It has been this way for almost two hundred years. And with every generation I am reborn as his vessel on earth."

Kemper turned to Megan. She felt his eyes ogling her. She didn't know how Darryl had transformed into Kemper, or where the other men had come from. The last thing she remembered was her neighbour, reaching for her. Nothing seemed tangible, like she was suspended outside her body, and as Kemper produced a large, knife from out of nowhere, she prayed her beliefs were true.

Ben saw the keen edge of Kemper's knife. "Don't you fucking touch her!" he screamed. "Megan! Nooo!"

The insane architect flashed Ben a sneer. The blade was poised over Megan's pale flesh.

"This is his house," Kemper said.

"Where he shall live evermore," the other thirteen resounded.

"Ben!" Megan cried.

Fear-tinged tears streamed from his wife's eyes. He had to stop this. He had to save her. She was all he had, and he hadn't understood that until now. The house had fed on his neglect.

He began to writhe and scream, twisting his arms and kicking out at Kemper's acolytes, but they might as well have been made of stone. Three of them made him stand and wrenched his arms behind his back. One of his shoulders tore from its socket. The reporter bit his tongue from the agony, and his mouth filled with blood at the very moment Kemper's knife kissed Megan's skin.

"Megan!"

The knife opened her abdomen in a horizontal incision.

Megan shrieked.

Ben screamed along with her. He pulled on his injured arm, dug in his heels and spat blood in his captor's faces, but their gazes were locked on the spectacle.

He collapsed to his knees in shock. He vomited. His blood and sputum coalesced with his wife's essence on the floor, while Megan's screams threatened to shatter his ear drums.

"This is his house," Kemper said, as he spread the edges of her wound apart. "Where he shall live forever more."

Ben lifted his head when Megan's screams ceased. "You fucking killed her..."

Kemper shook his head. "She lives. She is enamoured by His grace."

"Bear witness," the group rejoiced.

The house shook. The world shuddered beneath his feet. Dust showered from the walls, along with paintings and other ornaments. A china cabinet spilled its contents and fell with a great crash. The group of men stood still. Ben forced himself to rise. On unsteady feet he made a run for his wife, but Kemper blocked his path.

"Wait and see!" Kemper told him, knife in hand.

There was a violent crack of thunder and a flash of lightning and Ben looked skyward. The entire roof of the house was ripped away; it disintegrated into a million pieces. They were exposed to the blackest of nights, save for one distant white luminescence, which shone down, casting even darker shadows. The house stilled, and Ben dropped to his knees again.

Kemper stood at the end of the table and held his hands up to the light. "He is here!"

The house shifted, tilting at an angle so harsh that Ben fell on all fours. The house moved towards the light so fast, that for a moment all the air in room was lost. The reporter gasped in a lung full of air when the light came into colossal view, and he beheld the face of Kemper's god. The abomination was constructed of human souls tangled like twine, trapped in a sea of nothing. But that was false. There was a world inside the darkness, and Ben could see it all. Kemper's God lived in the house on the corner of Willow Street, and in the house on Mayne Avenue, but the construct was as expansive as heaven itself. Where Ben stood was not simply inside Kemper's House, but rather inside the temple; inside the God's soul.

Tears of trepidation rolled down Ben's cheeks as he stood at the temple's door and beheld its dark architecture. It was an homage to all the dark houses through time; every house, wherever an abomination had been committed or conceived. He saw rooms within rooms: attics with corpses resting on beds of lye, bedrooms with cupboards full of spindly fingers, basements wet with mildew and blood, spiral staircases adorned with the broken bodies of virgin brides.

Other buildings, too. Ben saw the West Plains hospital, and heard dying patients calling out Kemper's name. Through the coil of time, he was shown asylums full of men and women, pulling out their hair and muttering His name. Houses of horrors hatched inside the temple; Ben could smell death coming from each and every one.

The temple took hold of Ben's body and his feet left the floor. Paralysed, he floated through the insane construct and was forced to enter each house and room. In one, he saw a man in a Georgian wig and frock coat, garrotting his wife, a blank stare on his powdered face. In the basement of another, a timber house, surrounded by a woodland forest, were endless stacks of books for summoning the black God, each page scrawled with innocent blood. He witnessed torture in a nursery, torment in a master bedroom—all in the god's name.

Some houses were plain, others decadent, but they all bore the mark of Eric Kemper's God. The rooms orbited the deity like the dust of shattered moons. They were books on a shelf that the creature could indulge in whenever it pleased, to the calamity of all within. Ben was ushered into each and every one, and his mind was etched with every window, every door, and every death. He would have forgotten his own name inside the houses of the temple, if not for Kemper's voice, which eventually drew him away from its terrible visage.

"I live through him and he lives through me!"

The darkness surrounding the house bled inside, through the cracks in the windowsills, through gaps in the wood, and up through the floor. It snaked through Kemper's body and out of his eyes and mouth, where it coiled and caressed the wound in Megan's torso.

She came awake with a scream.

Megan contorted in agony, and her back arched as tendrils of blackness entered her body. Every blood vessel burned cold as the black void crept in, like ink infiltrating water. The great undulating face loomed over her and smiled. The human souls which comprised its lips rolled apart to make the gesture. They too wailed in pain, but their cries were soundless in the vastness of space.

The god's blood spread into Megan's mind and she was presented with countless images of humanity, suffering in the darkness of every house. The strobing sights left her paralysed and she succumbed, powerless to resist the god's infiltration. Her head lolled. Her husband struggled against the man who'd damned them all.

She shuddered briefly as the god's blood settled inside and watched as Kemper knocked Ben to the floor and straddled him, his knife raised. Kemper's followers looked on, but their visages had changed, and Megan saw the truth.

No longer were they men of aristocracy. She recognised the Campbell family from across the street—Max, Carol, Matthew and Zachary. An elderly couple stood beside them. She saw a young girl, and of course, Darryl. On the other side of the circle, were a mother and her son, another couple clasping hands, and one solitary man in a hospital gown. The god's blood told her who they were—all of them victims of the Kemper House, destined to stand in for the thirteen men who'd sacrificed themselves to Kemper's religion so many years ago. Megan watched as Kemper pressed the blade to Ben's cheek.

"There is nothing you can do," Kemper said to her husband.

Ben tried to move, but straining inched the blade closer to his eye, which ran freely with tears. "Please..." Ben said. "Please..."

"You can beg," Kemper sneered. "Or you can give yourself to him."

The dark god shivered in ecstasy at the possibility of another soul, and the wave radiated down into the house like an aftershock. Ben looked to the god and then to her. His eyes begging for *her* forgiveness.

She willed him to feel her but he turned away, back to the vile Kemper who waited so patiently.

"I'm not going to beg anymore." Ben said. He raised his knee and caught Kemper in the gut.

The architect wheezed and dropped his knife, but before Ben could get to his feet, the ghosts of Mitchell Cross and Darryl Novak pinned him to the floor. The spirits turned Ben on his back and held his wrists down.

An enraged Kemper drew a determined breath and grabbed the knife. This time there was no hesitation, and he inserted the tip of the knife into the corner of Ben's left eye. Unable to look away, Megan was forced to watch, and listen to her husband's screams as the knife slid slowly into his skull.

"I won't kill you," Kemper told Ben, who went limp and docile. "You will serve as a witness to this rebirth, the chronicler of a new age."

From the amount of blood on the knife, Megan discerned that Kemper had only inserted it far enough to incapacitate her husband, rather than kill him. But when Kemper, Cross and Darryl withdrew, she saw Ben lying on the floor, as good as dead, and she wished she was, too.

Kemper came to her side. He smiled, and the skin of his chest and arms cracked and split—a centuries-old husk that had reached its end.

"Behold the Mother of Darkness," he said, before falling to pieces.

His followers, the residents of Willow Street, encircled her and spoke as one.

"Behold the Mother of Darkness."

Megan picked up her bags and opened the front door. The early morning sun streamed in, and she blinked against the brightness of the new day. A breeze tousled her hair, and its pine scent reinvigorated her senses. She was ready to move on, and begin the next chapter of her life.

And yet, something didn't feel right.

Megan frowned at the odd sense of detachment she felt, but quickly put that down to the anxiety of taking the first step in a new direction. She stepped outside and closed the door to her old house. She checked her watch, expecting her cab to arrive at any moment. She saw the people from number 70 Willow Street, the two boys Matthew and Zachary, washing their father Max's truck and splashing water on one another. Max and his wife, Carol, stood on the lawn laughing at the boys' horseplay, as happy as any couple could be. A nice elderly couple, Richard and Maggie, walked past the Campbell's, offering the family a friendly wave.

Megan carried her bags to the kerb and looked farther up the street. At number 61 she saw Amy and Darryl. They were happily tending to their rose garden, the red and white blossoms shining in the mid-morning sun. Darryl was a ball of excitement as he showed Amy how to properly prune the rose bushes and make them glow. Clearly, they were living life to the fullest.

And yet, once again a twinge of uncertainty plagued her.

Megan shook her head as she looked back, eager to spy the cab. She smiled at her nervousness. She remembered she'd been that way too, when she'd left home to go to college, when she'd started her first job as a salesperson, and later when she'd got married...

The house across the street drew her attention, and she couldn't believe she hadn't seen it before. It was a gruesome building, with rotten walls and grimy windows, and the spire on the roof resembled a skeletal finger pointing to the sky. Everything about the house made Megan's skin crawl, and yet her neighbours on the street seemed oblivious to it.

It's just an old house, Besides, I'll be leaving all this behind any moment.

The distinctive yellow hue of the taxi caught her eye and she quickly hailed it. It pulled over to the side of the road. Even the driver wore a friendly smile.

"Where to, miss?"

"To the airport, please."

He got out and helped Megan put her bags in the trunk, and as she was opening one of the rear passenger doors, she felt the urge to look at the black house across the street once more.

A man stood at a window on the top floor. He was tall and handsome, but his face was stricken, and one of his eyelids drooped. The man pressed his palm to the glass, as if he was waving.

Megan quickly got inside the cab and told the driver she was ready to go. As she left Willow Street and its ugly black house, Megan gave the building no more thought and put the queasy movement in her stomach down to nothing more than nerves.

ACKNOWLEDGEMENTS

There are a number of people without whom *Hollow House* would not exist: my beta readers Amanda J. Spedding and Matthew Tait and of course, my editors, Janet J. Holden and Kate Jonez. Thank you all for helping me bring *Hollow House* to life.

ABOUT THE AUTHOR

Two-time international Bram Stoker Award-nominee®*, Greg Chapman is a horror author and artist based in Queensland, Australia.

Greg is the author of several novels, novellas and short stories, including his award-nominated debut novel, *Hollow House* and collections, *Vaudeville and Other Nightmares*, and *This Sublime Darkness and Other Dark Stories*.

He is also a horror artist and his first graphic novel *Witch Hunts: A Graphic History of the Burning Times*, (McFarland & Company) written by authors Rocky Wood and Lisa Morton, won the Superior Achievement in a Graphic Novel category at the Bram Stoker Awards® in 2013.

He was also the President of the Australasian Horror Writers Association from 2017-2020.

* Superior Achievement in a First Novel for *Hollow House* (2016) and Superior Achievement in Short Fiction, for "The Book of Last Words" (2019)

Curious about other Crossroad Press books?
Stop by our site:
http://store.crossroadpress.com
We offer quality writing
in digital, audio, and print formats.

www.ingramcontent.com/pod-product-compliance
Lightning Source LLC
Chambersburg PA
CBHW020640180626
46816CB00003B/1060